# Thomas Milton

# BLOOD OF

# NEW EDEN

Thomas Milton

ISBN: 0692680594

ISBN-13: 9780692680599

*For Arden :*

*Forevermore*

Thomas Milton

# Contents

# Acknowledgments

The author wishes to thank everyone who has helped with and supported this project and his exceptional crowd-funding patrons:

**FRIENDS**: Todd Beck; Shannon Rhodes; Allen and Nancy Edwards; Patrick Hoffman; Rodney Huffman; Nathan Lamb; Jesse Lawson; Brian Chilcher; Martina Martin; Tina Juras; Jessie and Jessica Martinez; Michael and Jenna Perkins.

<u>**FAMILY**</u>: Arden Goetz; Carla Walsh; Bekah and Rico Esquivel; Tom, Carol, and Jeff Goetz; Muriel Walsh and the author's father, Dean, and brother, William Walsh.

<u>*MUSES:*</u> Emluisa Collina; Heather Smith; Danielle St. Sauveur; and most certainly Dana "Chris" McLeod!

Blood of New Eden

Welcome to the ~~horrible~~ wonderful world of FleshArt

Remember: The Pain Stops…

Eventually…

But The Beauty Is Eternal

# PROLOGUE

*Art, like humor, can be found in anything…even death, so it's not unusual to blur the lines that divide all three or, even worse, sometimes confuse them for one another.*

It seemed like any other New Eden evening when Rosalee decided she would return to Manna, her art gallery, to finish paperwork. It was her least favorite part of running the business: the invoicing, payments, and licensing that went into owning a gallery was so much more than she had expected, but if she was to share her love and passion for art, she knew this was part of the deal.

Times weren't as they used to be, when you could simply display the paintings or lithographs of some young, up-and-coming talent and sell them for outrageous prices. No, those days were long gone. When the government of New Eden decreed that art was obsolete, most people gave up on their creations. It wasn't so much the threat of being penalized by law, which you could be, (according to the fear-mongering media); no one could honestly tell you of someone he *knew* had run into trouble for putting pen to paper or brush to canvas. But people were distracted by their holoscreens, by the games they played with one another without leaving their homes, and by a new set of mind-numbing, highly euphoric drugs that were gaining popularity in all classes and castes of modern society.

Only the elite and those with a true interest in art would pay the fees to be properly licensed. Few people had sufficient passion left in anything to be dedicated enough to own a gallery. In the city-state known as CS214, there were probably only half a dozen "legal" galleries—one of them Rosalee's. Others could be found in the slums, but the slums were closed off to the rest of the world...the world of CS214.

Rosalee felt pretty good as she walked the short distance from her apartment to the gallery. The wet, shimmering, and slick streets reflected the light of every building like a muddled mirage of color. The beauty of this caught her. She had dosed up less than an hour earlier, and it gave her the energy to brave the late-night chill to tackle something as mundane as paperwork. There were few cars outside, and even fewer people. This solitude and the mechanized hum of the city were appealing on these late-night jaunts. It was soothing, this din of machines and electronics toiling away in unison to keep the city-state and its citizens in regulation. Everything in this day and age moved in a fluid synchronicity, thanks in part to the effort and wisdom of the past and its people. Truly, these were days of comfort and luxury. Almost everyone was imprinted with the knowledge necessary for the task, the job, or the skill he or she was genetically bred to do, but there was no longer the feeling of work or labor. "We each have a purpose, something that we were literally born to do," someone had told her once. Rosalee was born to be an exhibitor; even in this day of suppressed natural talent, people wanted to believe in the magic of art.

She walked between the rows of houses that morphed into stand-alone buildings. The gallery was at the end of the block. It was an unassuming building with walls of white brick interspersed with large glass panels to make sure what was displayed inside could be seen from the street. The exhibition was a new one for her, only a week old, and in her fourteen years of running the gallery, this was the first time she had nerve enough to put something so taboo, so controversial on display. Patronage was waning, and she didn't need much convincing when the strange but affluent gentleman known to her only as Rikoh strolled in on a slow afternoon ten days earlier. At first, she didn't know what to make of him. A tall, thin man with short, slicked, black hair and sharp facial features, he was quite handsome. He wore what was obviously a very expensive black suit. In fact, his entire demeanor—his gait, his gaze—seemed almost mechanized, but no android existed that was so utterly real. On that day, Rikoh, as he called himself, proposed to Rosalee his idea of a new exhibition, one that would, as he put it, "change the way the world looked at life." The audacity of his idea shocked her, but since he was willing to finance the exhibit with more money than she hoped to make in a good year, much of what seemed uncouth became more appealing. Once the initial pieces were set and Rikoh had given his approval, she saw very little of him. He paid up front, in cash, and Rosalee had no doubt that this mysterious stranger had quite a cache of money stockpiled. It didn't matter to her if he was honest or a crook, for he had done nothing wrong. Still, the theme of the exhibition had made her uneasy, but her fears quickly faded at the grand opening. Never in anyone's memory had there been such a turnout for an art installation.

Rosalee could now see into the gallery, and she noted the up-lit signs that described each of the pieces: crime-scene photographs of infamous murders, pictures of past "serial killers," cases containing weapons and artifacts from the sites of the most horrendous atrocities committed in the twentieth century—the worst cases of man's inhumanity to man. It was an exhibition of horrors the likes of which hadn't been seen in hundreds of years. The very idea of a human killing another human for the pleasure of it had been erased even before the Great Continental Divide, and now that people were genetically tailored to be the best humans they could be, modern society had no room for crimes such as murder or rape. There was still a need for lawfulness in New Eden, as every society needs to have rules, and so there was still an active police force. But violent person-on-person crimes were nearly extinct. If it weren't for the violence still seen in the slums, one could safely assume than man had "learned his lesson" and the futility of interpersonal violent crime was assured.

Rosalee walked up to the glass doors of the gallery's entrance and put her hand in the biometric

ID scanner. She heard the quiet ticking sound of the door's locks disengaging. The glass doors opened automatically, and she stepped into the warmth and dryness of her gallery. As she took off her jacket, she heard a familiar voice.

"GOOD EVENING, MISS SANCHEZ."

It was the voice of MELaNie, the building's computer support system.

"Hello, MEL," said Rosalee. "Just coming in to get caught up on paperwork. How're things?"

"EVERYTHING IS 100 PERCENT OPERATIONAL, MISS SANCHEZ," replied the low, programmed voice. "ROOM TEMPERATURE IS SET TO SIXTY-SIX DEGREES. I HAVE NO INDICATION OF FAULTS OR ALARMS ON THE PREMISES."

"That's good, MEL," said Rosalee. "Could you please set low-lighting preset number two?"

Upon that request, the building became slightly more illuminated. It took on a pleasant, warm glow. Rosalee hung her jacket on a metal peg on the wall. She walked across the open floor, heading to her office behind the white, brick partition. It was then she noticed a strange odor. As Rosalee turned into her office, she gasped and staggered back in horror at the sight she had just seen. Tears of fear began to run down her face, and the gasp gave way to a scream. She turned and ran out the front door into the night. Behind her, a pool of blood oozed slowly across the threshold of her office.

# ONE

Buzzz!

Simon's eyelids fluttered open, but everything was still a blur. The comedown from IT had started to kick in, and someone wasn't being very nice by ringing him at this time of morning. Simon was grossly aware of the pulse thudding in his head, but it wasn't until he tried to move his arms to rub the sleep from his eyes that he came face-to-face with the sensation that he was all too familiar with: pain. Every joint and muscle felt as if it had been roasting overnight; every nerve was alive with electrical pinpricks that radiated shudders throughout his naked, battered body.

Buzzz!

"Yeah, just a minute!" shouted Simon, turning his head to see the dull screen of the videophone flashing the message: Incoming call. Do you accept?

"For fuck's sake," Simon thought as he willed his broken, scarred, and calloused body to roll to the side of the bed. "This better be pretty goddamned important."

He sat up on the edge of the bed with a groan and loud pops and cracks from forty years of treating his body like shit. Anne used to tell him he just "enjoyed life too much." She was right; she was always right. As Simon touched the hidden button to bring the table lamp up to a dull glow, he caught a glimpse of her picture in its jeweled, silver frame, which was engraved with FOREVER and ALWAYS. Anymore, it seemed like a sick joke that mocked him. It wasn't her fault, and God knows he had tried his best. It was after the fight, after she'd up and left him, accusing him of an affair that wasn't real. The affair never happened, but his late nights at work and constant departures from home only promoted his sweet Anne's doubts about his fidelity. Doubts which, Simon always suspected, had been fanned by one of Anne's friends, a scorned shrew of a woman who wouldn't trust a man if her life depended on it. But it wasn't this nameless "friend," and it wasn't the fight that tore him up so; it was that he never had the chance to apologize and set things straight. She disappeared that night, never to be seen again. The pain would never get any better, and Simon had come to accept that in the five years since. The only thing that made it tolerable was the IT.

He picked up the small, cylindrical, surgical-steel tube that lay on the nightstand and checked the green indicator on the back. He had remembered to leave himself a fully loaded cartridge of IT the night before. Sometimes he would forget, and the tube was left empty, causing rushes of fear and paranoia to claw at him. Today would be a better day. He turned the small dial on the front to the number 4 position; held the tube up to his hairless chest, pushing down hard on the skin atop of where his heart should be; and pressed the button on the back of the tube.

Almost instantaneously, Simon felt the sharp pierce of the tiny needle that flew into his chest and withdrew, but not without delivering a four-microgram dose of IT straight into his heart. Within the span of two heartbeats, everything that had been hurting suddenly ceased to. The fog in his brain lifted and was replaced by a warm, glowing feeling. He was alert and ready to disguise himself as a normal person once again…at least for the next twelve hours or so. He managed a smirk and rolled his head around, causing an obscene number of cracks and pops in his neck, but he felt no pain. In fact, he was feeling good. Even the sorrow of missing his dear Anne, while still there, was dulled enough that he could push it aside once again, bury it for a little while longer as he got through the day.

Simon pushed the button on the videophone to accept the call. The text on the screen switched to AUDIO ONLY/VIDEO MUTE (he never accepted a live video from someone he didn't know, not at this, his private home number).

"Yeah, can I help you?" Simon asked.

The voice on the other end was a flat baritone, firm and confident. "Good evening—or should I say morning?—Mr. Topaz. My name is Rikoh. I have an urgent business matter I would like to discuss with you. I request that you be at your office and available in one hour. Thank you."

With a beeping sound and before Simon could even say, "What's this all about?" the screen of the videophone flashed CALL ENDED.

"Asshole," Simon muttered.

The clock on the screen read 4:07 a.m. Simon shook his head, stood up from the bed, and walked into the bathroom. He pulled the fader switch just inside the bathroom door up to the indented number three position. The light was dim, but it was bright enough that he could make out the layout of the bathroom, not that it ever changed. A typical modern apartment bathroom, with a shower stall to his left, a toilet on the back wall, and a counter with a built-in sink to his right. On the wall above the counter stretched a mirror. A medicine cabinet faced him from the right-angled *L* formed by the edge of the counter. On the opposite wall was a touch-screen control pad. Most people simply spoke to their automated comfort-living systems, but Simon was never comfortable with the feeling that someone was watching his every move, so all of the audio command and response systems throughout his apartment had been muted but listening.

He always kept the water temperature in the shower the same: cold. The IT made his skin sensitive to heat, and trying to shave with hot water would cause more pain on the comedown. Once, while he was high on IT, his skin was so numb that he had scalded himself with the heat, and since the cold water felt only of moisture, it was safest to leave it running cold. He jumped into the shower for a few minutes and then went back to the sink to shave. It was with the towel around his waist that he first took a good look at his face in the mirror.

Simon had a kind and handsome face, but one that also reflected his sadness and longing. His pupils were wide open, a side effect of the IT, and one he desperately tried to hide by wearing contact lenses. His contacts made his eyes appear a normal, dark-emerald color, but they also served another function. When he blinked, a small message in the lower right-hand corner of his eye simply stated ACTIVE. He finished his daily cleansing ritual in a matter of minutes and went back to the bedroom to grab his clothes from the closet. It was simple uniform of slacks, shoes, and a collarless, white, button shirt, which he left untucked. His hair was short enough that he simply patted it down before putting on his jacket and arming himself with provisions he'd need for the day: his wallet, his phone, his green pearl-handled knife/good-luck charm, his dosing pen, and a small metal box containing four vials of IT, which he put in a hidden pocket on the inside of his jacket. Forty minutes after the phone awoke him, Simon was ready to head downstairs and find out what this "Rikoh guy" wanted.

***

Simon's office was four floors below his apartment in the same building. Simon lived, worked, and (sometimes) played out of an old converted hotel, once one of the nicest hotels on the coast, but in the years following the Great Continental Divide, technology had made taking a holiday almost obsolete.

In New Eden, there were six teracomplexes: massive, sprawling campuses that stretched into the sky like the pyramids of ancient, long-forgotten civilizations. As tall as the teracomplexes were, they took up six times as much ground space—some even overlapping the edge of the ocean. Each one housed and employed many citizens of New Eden. They were giant, multilevel malls combined with areas committed to factory work, medicine, pleasure, and residences. There were still plenty of stand-alone houses and buildings outside the teracomplexes, which were occupied mostly by the elite. And then there were the slums—the proverbial "wrong side of the tracks" shantytowns that were mostly underground with high security walls on the surface level. The walls had been erected not only to give the illusion that proper, law-abiding people were safe from whatever nefarious activity took place inside them, but also for aesthetics. The walls gave the landscape the look of proper control, order, and conformity.

In the middle of City-State 214 was a giant pyramid-shaped building made of gold and glass. This was the home of the exalted leader. An enigma of a man with no other name, he was called, simply, "Leader." His face was well known, as were the slogans of propaganda on every video screen around CS214. (Drink this; Leader does…Eat this; Leader does…Wear this; it's Leader approved!) The fact that Leader's face was only seen *with* a product—he was never enjoying it, never consuming it, never wearing it—was lost on the majority of the populous. The fact that Leader had never been seen in public was also ignored. The good people of CS214 felt protected under Leader's watchful and kind-looking face. It was a regal face that commanded respect, but it seemed as compassionate as it was handsome.

The building where Simon worked and lived

was somewhere between social classes. It wasn't as mundane as the teracomplexes were, but it wasn't a run-down slum shanty either. The building was an old, unassuming structure, maybe twenty stories high. It was not much wider a than any old skyscraper. Of the top ten stories in the residential area, only four floors were occupied; and on those floors, each resident pretty much had the entire level to himself. Simon had money but was by no means rich or a member of the elite class. There was quite a bit of empty space on his floor, but it was a classical style of living. Most people preferred living in the teracomplexes for the convenience and because the government promoted those who would live there. The government provided residents with just about any modern luxury they could want, not to mention the efficiency of never having to travel far to be anywhere they wanted or were obligated to be.

Simon didn't crave all that opulence because of the events surrounding Anne's disappearance and because he was one of the few people left who were naturally born, meaning that he had a real mother and father. He'd lost both at an early age due to the second plague: a virus that was never fully understood and that thinned the population of the planet. Where once there was overpopulation and more than twelve billion people trying to cram themselves onto what little real estate there was, now there were only about 500 million people. No one knew for sure just how many people were left on the planet, but if more people were out there, one would never know it judging from the empty, lonely streets.

Simon's office was typical. There was a small reception area with a couch on one wall and a couple of leather chairs on the other. Between the seats were small, glass tables bearing cheap electronic readers, each flashing the covers of all of the popular magazines: *Time*, *Omni*, *CS214 NewsFeed*, and *HoloLeisure Monthly*. On the table in the corner sat a videophone with a small plastic plaque that read NEW EDEN CALLS ONLY. (It was damned expensive to call any of the other islands: South Eden, Euroasia, Afrika, or Oceania, and Simon wasn't going to foot the bill for those calls, or, God forbid, an exorbitantly priced off-world call.) A desk sat in the reception area, and TriXie sat behind it. TriXie was the newest in robotic personal assistants with billions of preprogrammed actions and responses for interacting with Simon and his clients. The Tri-X series had always been the most friendly and realistic-looking line of assistants, this side of owning an actual android. But androids cost much more than Simon ever wanted to spend. It was rare to see an android other than, maybe, a butler at an elitist's house or a guard at Leader's Great Pyramid.

When Simon walked into the office, a tall, thin man greeted him. This man was adorned with sharp features, and he wore a black suit, a black shirt, and a white tie. He was impeccably dressed—there was not a loose button, a scuff, or a piece of lint to be seen on his person. He stood up from the leather chair when TriXie said, "GOOD MORNING, SIMON. YOU HAVE A GUEST, A RIKOH WAITING."

"I can see that. Thank you, TriXie," said Simon, never taking his eyes off Rikoh.

13

"Thank you for seeing me on such short notice, Mr. Topaz," Rikoh said.

"I didn't seem to have much choice," Simon said jokingly.

Rikoh did not react. There was no smile or grin, no sympathy or apology, not even a handshake.

"Indeed," said Rikoh. "Time is urgent and of the essence. Mr. Topaz, may we please speak in your office?"

"Of course." Simon led Rikoh through a single door into his office. It was a wide room with an ornate, wooden desk against the back wall. A bottled ship, a scrimshawed horn, old clocks that no longer ran, and other nineteenth- and twentieth-century relics sat on wooden pedestals with glass domes on the west side of the room. On the east side, there was another leather couch, much nicer than the one in the reception area. On the east wall of the office a line of cabinets with a sink and bottles of different liquors in a shiny silver rack were on display. Simon gestured to the liquor.

"Can I get you something to drink, Mr. Rikoh?"

"No," Rikoh said flatly. He was investigating the different antiques. "I see you are a collector."

"Of sorts," said Simon.

"I am too. Let me be candid and to the point. I run an art exhibit downtown, at an art gallery called Manna. You may have heard of it. 'Twentieth-Century Horrors: Man's Inhumanity to Man.'"

"Yeah," Simon said. "I've been meaning to check it out. I hear you have some pretty fascinating things on display."

"Indeed, I do," Rikoh said. "Last evening, the gallery's owner, a Ms. Rosalee Sanchez, discovered a body in her office when she went in after hours."

"Sounds like a matter for the police." Simon motioned to one of two brown leather chairs that faced his desk. "Please, have a seat."

"Thank you," Rikoh said as he unbuttoned his jacket and sat down.

Simon sat in a large, brown leather chair behind his desk.

"Yes, it *is*, in fact, a matter for the police," Rikoh said, "and they are on the scene as we speak. I wish to hire you to find a missing artifact that was stolen during the break-in last night, but given the nature of it, I need the utmost discretion. I am told you are most effective in dealing with matters of a sensitive and secretive nature."

"Then you also know that my services are not cheap."

"Money is no object. Whatever the fee is, you will be paid; but I need to find my artifact and quickly. Can I count on you, Mr. Topaz?"

"I guess that depends," Simon said.

"Depends on what?"

"It depends entirely on what I'm looking for and what risk there is in getting it back."

"Then perhaps a visit to the scene of the crime would help to clarify matters."

"Perhaps."

Simon considered it. "Why not?" he thought. "At worst, I'll spend a couple hours with this prick; at best, I could make a tidy sum—the guy is obviously loaded."

"Why not?" Simon said as he stood to grab a jacket from the wall. "I've been wanting to see this exhibit anyway. What's better than a personal tour and getting in free, eh?"

Again, Rikoh was not amused. He stood and began walking out of the office with Simon right behind him.

"I do not know the risk you'll encounter, Mr. Topaz. But know this: even if you find my artifact simply lying on the street, you will be handsomely rewarded."

"That *is* good to know," said Simon.

He walked out to the reception area behind Rikoh.

"TriXie," he said, "I'll be out of the office for a few hours. Please set security to mode two."

"YES, MR. TOPAZ," the electronic voice said.

He walked out the door and into the elevator, where Rikoh was already waiting. As the elevator descended to the ground level, Simon asked, "So, if my discreet manner is so great, how is it that you found me?"

"I am well connected in society, Mr. Topaz. Upon consulting many people, your name came up as one of the best."

"Only *one of*?" Simon grinned as the elevator door opened. "I must be losing my touch."

# TWO

Rain fell and dawn was just breaking as Simon pulled up in front of Manna Gallery, where Rikoh's exhibit was housed. The police had already sealed off and evacuated every adjacent building. Simon looked up at the entrance. Other than the signs of a police presence (a few uniformed officers looking for clues; two men in trench coats talking to an attractive, young woman who was visibly shaken and upset; and the laser NO ENTRY tape that surrounded the building) one wouldn't suspect anything had happened here.

"A bit too much attention for a petty robbery," Simon thought. "Something else is going on."

"Come with me, Mr. Topaz."

Rikoh had slid in and stood just behind Simon's shoulder, and Simon was startled when he heard the request. Simon had a sixth sense about his surroundings, but Rikoh moved stealthily like a phantom.

"This way," said Rikoh as he motioned toward the only checkpoint into and out of the gallery.

Simon's contacts adjusted to the light, documenting everything he saw. The men approached the checkpoint, where a large, uniformed officer stood. The uniform was meant to intimidate. It was entirely black with a single glowing, blue stripe that ran across the armor-plated jacket and pants and a tactical helmet than only left the ape-man's square jaw exposed. He nodded at Rikoh, and it seemed like everything was in the right, but with one glance at Simon, he shot out his massive arm to block their entry.

"I'm sorry, sir, but this is an active crime scene. No guests are permitted," the cop said.

Simon wasn't sure of the cop's name, but "Smith" was embroidered on the breast of his jacket. Rikoh, not the least bit intimidated, responded with a low, calm growl.

"This is Mr. Topaz, my security detail. I have cleared it with Detective Riley."

Simon's heart fell; he was starting to think he was getting in over his head.

Simon glared at Rikoh, wondering what other unpleasant surprises the man had neglected to mention.

"Well, welly, well, well..."

A heavyset man, looking unkempt and disheveled in a black suit, white shirt, black bow tie, and a long, soaked trench coat, was addressing them. Simon knew the face of his onetime associate well enough. "They're fine, Smith," Detective Mark Riley said with a smirk as he slowly walked toward the gate. "Finey, fine, fine...eh?" He looked Simon up and down. "But not so fine, are we, Sy. Nope, in fact you look like...absolute shit." Riley chuckled.

Simon had known Mark since they were both in the academy together many years prior and at one time would have called the man his best friend. That was until Simon was dismissed from the force, having tested positive for IT. Simon had picked up the IT habit in the hospital during many months of rehabilitation as he recovered from the tortures that the Sindel Cartel had inflicted on him.

Simon had been deep undercover, investigating an illegal IT manufacturing and distribution ring. He had just enough concrete evidence to bring it down, when his cover was blown by someone inside the force. Simon could never prove it was Riley, but he had his suspicions—partly because Riley was the only one who knew that Simon was taking street-level IT to maintain his credibility in front of the cartel members and partly because Riley had received a sudden financial windfall not long after Simon was found in the waterfront warehouse fire. The initial reports were that Simon had died from his injuries, but this was just a ruse to lull Sindel and his men into a false sense of security. No one but the higher-ups knew of Simon's vitality, and it was quite a dramatic shock in the courtroom the day Simon took the stand to testify about what he'd been part of. After the sentencing, Sindel's men were put in an isolated cryostasis facility far away from CS214, and, in a karmic act of justice, a rival gang member assassinated Sindel.

The combination of Anne's disappearance only two years prior and the physical shock of being electrocuted, eviscerated, and burned alive by Sindel compelled Simon to lean more and more on IT to get through the pain every day. When he failed to show up to work and then tested positive, he knew it was the end of his career in public service. Because of the circumstances, the higher-ups allowed him to retire, citing his eyesight (and pain) as a permanent disability. Since then, Simon had made a decent career as a private investigator. Even he was surprised by how many people needed covert services done with discretion and no public record.

"How've you been, Mark?" Simon asked Riley.

"Eh…can't complain. Ever since ol' Uncle Joe died and left me everything, I just try to ride the desk unless it's sumthin', ya know, real important-like."

Simon knew from the sensors in his contacts that there was stress in Riley's voice. Some or maybe all of what Mark had just said was a lie. Simon didn't need a machine to know that, but he could care less about trying to dissect the meaning in Riley's statement.

"I got ta tell ya, Sy, when Mr. Rikoh said you were in charge of his security, I was a bit suspicious. But you know da protocol; don't fucks with me, and I won't fucks wit' chew."

Simon nodded in agreement.

"Anyways," continued Riley, "Rikoh tells me you're here to look into a missing personal item of his. But if happens to cross up with the murder investigation, I wanna know everything, a'right?"

The shock on Simon's face upon hearing the word "murder" was evident enough that Rikoh felt the need to respond. "Thank you, Detective Riley. We assure you our interest here is only an internal security matter. This other unfortunate incident…

Well, I'm sure will be well handled by our fine police department."

"Yeah, we will. Anyways, best I show you inside what we've got so far."

Riley motioned to the door and led the other two men into the gallery.

Once inside, Simon's eyes caught details of the notorious exhibit. Large photographs of crime scenes were hung on white walls. Underneath each was a red jewel, which he knew to be the sensor for the *Augmented Reality* experience. For a price, not only could patrons view these horrible testaments in a static image, but they could also put on a specially designed helmet that placed them at the event. Where possible, old video and photographic footage was used to capture every gory detail. If they were unsure of the details, the programmers of the exhibit would take creative license. But the results were the same: the viewer had the total sensory experience of being in the room right after a horrible crime was committed—everything from the Manson Family murders to the infamous gas chambers of Auschwitz. Nothing was considered too taboo to give the patron anything less than the total "death experience."

Among the pictures and laid out sporadically in the middle of the room were glass cases containing relics of human horror: prisoners' garb from a Nazi German concentration camp, a paint set used by convicted child-killer John Wayne Gacy, Chilean dictator General Pinochet's wheelchair, and other murder weapons and artifacts of the time. Simon was awestruck—not so much by the subject matter as by the grand scale of it all. In this room lived the legacies of a relatively small number of men (and women) who took the lives of many others in some of the worst possible ways the human brain can reason.

A tall, thin man wearing a blue raincoat with the gold letters LAB stenciled on the back approached from across the room.

"Excuse me, Detective Riley. We're ready to map the room."

Riley turned, looking at Simon but talking to Rikoh. "About fuckin timey time," he mumbled. "Pardon me, guys; I must attend to this."

Rikoh made a slight motion, which Simon guessed was the mechanical man's effort to nod. Simon wandered over to the closest display case to take a better look at what he was in for. Inside the case, a pair of bloody scissors rested next to a photo of two bodies in night apparel, one male and one female, lying in bed, as if ready to sleep. But eyes and eyelids of both figures were missing. Deep pools of red-black filled the orbits of their eyes, and streaks of blood ran down their faces like crimson tears. Reading the caption, Simon knew he had never heard of this couple or their demented son, a child of sixteen who, in a tantrum of spoiled rage, had drugged and murdered his parents using the very scissors that lay here now by pulling their eyes out with delicate precision and then severing the optic nerve from the brain. A family member found the grisly scene and then discovered the young lad sitting quietly at a table in the basement drawing pencil sketches of animals. In a dozen glass jars on the table were the dismembered eyes of his parents, of his missing toddler brother and sister, and of dozens of dogs, cats, and other animals from the area. Arguably the most disturbing find, however, was the large jar in the middle of the table. Floating in it were the sexual organs of his family members: his father's penis and scrotum; his mother's clitoris, labia, and nipples; and the same of his younger brother and sister. All supposedly removed with the same pair of shears.

As Simon finished reading the caption describing the incident, what should have been repulsion turned to curiosity. Simon stared at the infamous scissors, the contacts in his eyes taking measurements and light-sensitivity readings. Again, he didn't need the aid of a computer to tell him that something wasn't right. The light mounted on the inside of the case was beaming on the stainless steel, but there was no hint of reflection, no shadow.

"You have quite the eye, Mr. Topaz."

Rikoh walked over to the display, never once looking inside.

"Those scissors…they're fake," said Simon. "I mean, they're not made of a normal metal, are they?"

"Correct. It's a polymer that looks and feels just like metal, but the manufacturer hasn't discovered how to get light to properly diffuse and reflect. The real ones were encased in the vault behind Ms. Sanchez's office. Even she is not aware they are there."

Simon glanced up at Rikoh, a puzzled look on his face.

"Then all of these—"

Before he could finish, Rikoh completed the

sentence. "Are actually real. Yes, Mr. Topaz, this is the only mock-up in the entire exhibit. It was done for security's sake. Many times over the years, these shears have been a delectable temptation for collectors, especially FleshArtists who are looking for quite the inspirational tool."

Simon shook his head. He was familiar with the new fad of FleshArt. Ever since cloning replacement body parts became legal, many "donors" gave up their unwanted or malfunctioning body parts to a new breed of surgeon, the FleshArtist, in order to justify getting a newer, better part for their bodies. The money that an average donor could make would more than pay for the replacement, and with pharmaceutical-grade IT, there was little to no pain involved in either procedure. Cloning whole humans, however, was still highly illegal and considered unethical planet wide.

Simon noted one word in Rikoh's statement and did not hesitate to call him on it.

"What do you mean 'were' encased in the vault?"

Rikoh's lip curled up; it was the best the man could do to manage to smile.

"Indeed, Mr. Topaz, you are as good as I was told you would be. The shears, the real ones, as you would call them, are in a velvet-lined wooden box. This is what is missing following last night's...event, and this is what I hired you to find and return to me."

"Speaking of last night's event," Simon said. "Ms. Sanchez's office and the vault, may we see those?"

"This way."

Rikoh pointed toward the large, white, brick partition at the end of the room. He started walking toward it, and Simon followed. As Simon got closer, he smelled a stench he didn't like but was all too familiar with…the smell of rotting flesh. The majority of police personnel were at this end of the gallery, focused on whatever was inside, behind that wall. They didn't have to get much closer before Simon saw the blood on the floor. A clearly defined pool, it had been sitting for hours. Rikoh stopped at the edge of the small crowd, and Simon moved along behind it until he finally saw what all the commotion was about.

Riley smirked. "Youse look likes you've never seen a dead body before."

"No, I have," Simon said with a sigh. "But just not in so many pieces."

# THREE

Halfway across town, in an affluent part of CS214, Dr. Brian Douglas was waking up and going through his normal morning routine. His daily ritual had always been the same: a five-mile jog around the neighborhood; a fifteen-minute shower; and a light breakfast of juice, hard-boiled eggs, and dry toast. For Brian, there was comfort in routine. Although his ID said he was fifty years old, he had the body of a twenty-year-old Adonis. In fact, it was only near his eyes that he showed any sign of aging.

Brian did his best to take care of himself. It wasn't vanity, which he had in droves, but more an interest in keeping his blood pure. He didn't want to chance mingling his blood with that of a lesser person—lesser in both attractiveness and intellect. As he was reading the news headlines on his handheld holoscreen, his videophone started to beep. He picked up the receiver, never once looking at the screen. Only a few people had this number, and fewer still would dare to call him even if it was an emergency. But this was a call he had been expecting.

"Yes?" Brian asked.

A raspy, worn-out voice replied, "It's done. I left a parcel in your basement. A token of my esteem."

"What about the gallery?"

"I gave them something else…something better to look at."

"No one I know, I hope."

"Since when has *that* ever been a concern, my good doctor?"

Brian laughed. "When will I see you again?" he asked.

"Later…Chris is bringing me a new client, and I'm feeling quite inspired."

"Ah, very good," Brian muttered. "Very good, indeed."

"I shall let you know more, Doctor, after my consultation. Enjoy your gift."

With that and the sound of a double beep, the call was ended. Brian finished his breakfast and closed the holoscreen. He went back to his bedroom to get dressed: black slacks, a white dress shirt, and a black tie—a nondescript outfit to adorn his tanned, muscular frame. He made his way to the basement stairs. There were doors at both ends, and the stone stairway automatically lit up when he entered. The door at the bottom of the stairs was brushed steel with no handles, only a bioreactive panel. Brian put his hand on it, and the door opened with barely a whisper. He walked inside, and the entire room began to glow.

The room was covered in sterile, white, plastic laminate, like opaque Teflon, lit from behind. Along the west wall, a stainless-steel counter traveled the length of the room, with cabinets above and below. In the middle of the room was an autopsy table made of white ceramic and equipped with arm, leg, and neck restraints.

On the table sat what looked to be a wooden box wrapped in butcher paper.

"Nice touch," Brian thought.

He carefully unwrapped the paper to find the wooden display box, which was clasped in the front. He undid the clasp and looked inside. Before him lay the weapon that was involved in the infamous twentieth-century Blithe family murder. He picked up the scissors by the handles to get a better look at them. The ends were covered in dried blood. Satisfied, Brian put the scissors back in their case and closed the clasp. He carried the box over to a wall, where he pressed on a section of the white plastic. A small drawer, hidden in the paneling, opened. He placed the box inside and pushed again on the same area.

"Enough fun for today," he thought. "Time to get to work."

Brian went to the far wall and touched a large panel of the white plastic. He heard a click, and the panel moved automatically inward and to the left to nest inside the wall. Behind the panel was a small washroom with sink, mirror, shower, and a few pegs on the wall. On one peg was a white, full-body, sterile suit with boots and a cowl sewn into the satin nanofabric. A Velcro patch sealed the crotch front, and a plastic zipper ran the rest of the way, from just below the beltline to underneath the chin. On the next peg hung a clear plastic bag containing cotton glove liners, nitrile gloves, and a red silk face mask with eyeholes cut out. Each was in a separate, sealed, and sterile compartment. On a third peg hung a black rubber smock and a plastic face shield.

Brian undressed until he was fully nude, folding his clothes neatly and leaving them on the small cabinet next to the sink. Inside the open cabinet, which only came to waist height, were shelves containing top-of-the-line men's grooming products. Just to the left of the faucet, on the sink, sat an empty drinking glass. On the right was a bottle of mood-stabilizing pills. Brian took two of the pills from the bottle, put them in his mouth, and held them between his front teeth. He held the glass under the tap, filling it about a quarter of the way; let the pills slide into his mouth; and chased them down with a gulp of water. He set the glass down on the sink and stared at his nude body in the mirror. He was tanned, muscular, hairless, and well endowed.

Within seconds, a sudden wave of euphoria and calmness settled over his body. He blinked and stared at himself again. He was comfortable and sedate enough to know that what he was about to do wouldn't faze him in the least. He put on the sterile suit, gloves, smock, and face mask; and walked back into the main room. He touched the spot that had removed the door to the washroom, and the plastic panel slid back into its original place, causing the washroom to vanish.

Brian walked over to the long steel counter, placed his hands on it, and pushed down near the edge with his finger. As he did so, a rectangular video screen appeared on the counter, its size determined by the placement of his fingers. On the screen were buttons labeled Music, Lights, and Temperature, among other gauges and meters. For each button he touched, a submenu appeared. He turned on the music—classical strings and piano—volume low. He set the lighting in the room to a dim glow, extinguishing the backlights behind the wall panels, and leaving only the floor illumination and a garish, white light that highlighted the autopsy table. He set the temperature to be cold enough to kill germs and bacteria, but warm enough that he couldn't see his breath. With a swipe of his hand, the screen disappeared.

    Brian opened the closet at the end of the counter. He rolled out a cart of covered surgical instruments and set it next to the autopsy table. From a cupboard and a cabinet, he pulled out a bag of saline solution and a bag type-O blood. He attached the leads to an automatic drip machine, the output of which was still sealed. He rolled out another cart from an opposing cabinet that contained a half dozen different-sized syringes. Finally, he opened a drawer beneath the sink that contained vials of different liquid medications, the most notable of which was a small, fluorescent-green vial containing concentrated IT. A dosing gun lay in the same drawer, and while Brian put the other drugs on the cart with the syringes, he put the vial of IT into the rear of the dosing gun. Flicking the safety lever with his thumb, he pushed a button on the side of the gun, and with a pneumatic whoosh, a needle pierced the top of the vial, draining half the contents into the gun. A small green level indicator showed the gun to be primed, full, and armed. He was ready.

Brian walked over to a corner of the room and put one hand on the wall with the hidden washroom and the other on the wall to the right. With a whir, the white, plastic panel split in two—each side sliding forward and then parting to make an entryway. The opening was not much taller than Brian was, only about six and a half feet high, and just under three feet wide. It led to complete blackness. He touched a button on the inside of the wall, and torch-like sconces lit up dimly and flickered—a gothic touch he had added just to indulge his morbid fantasy.

Inside, the small room smelled dank, and the stone floor was wet from a continuous sheet of running water that came from a long slit along the bottom of the right-hand wall and drained into grates on the opposite side of the room, underneath a massive iron and steel cage. Inside the cage were two figures: one the remnants of what used to be a man, at least some humanoid figure with a male penis, but to say it was now a corpse would be doing it honor. The carcass was carelessly piled up in the corner of the cage, no life, and thus no threat to anyone, so Brian paid little attention to it. What was unremarkable to Brian, but would add to his mythology when this heap was later found, was the precision of the evisceration – not all of the skin or muscle was removed, just deliberate sections, the eyes, the scalp, and some in geometric patterns, others with a more "flamboyant" flair…"the artist's cut" as it was known in the ranks of FleshArtists and their patrons.

Brian's attention was more on the other body in the room: a thin, muscular woman who was chained to the wall; her hands were shackled at her sides to the same stone wall that restrained her feet. Two leather straps were bolted to the wall. One cinched at her hips, and the other, across her breasts; a third strap held her head against the wall. A gag was strapped around her mouth.

She was asleep, and it wasn't until Brian unlocked and opened the door of the cage that she came to. She saw him moving toward her through tear-reddened eyes. Not quite aware of what was happening, but ever so frightened by this massive figure wearing a black rubber smock. His face was hidden behind a featureless red cloth; all she could see were his eyes, his brown soulless eyes. Before she could manage a scream, he lunged toward her, and she felt the cold pierce of the dosing gun against her neck. In an instant, there was no longer any fear or pain. She was completely numb and relaxed. Even as he unhooked the straps, freeing her from the wall, she made no effort to fight him. She thought she felt him pick her up and carry her from the room, and then she lost consciousness.

When she awoke, she found herself strapped down to the ceramic table with a foam cushion underneath her head. She was naked, and all of the hair on her scalp, her eyebrows, and her sex seemed to have been shaved off. A faint whisper of classical music was playing in the background. She was cold but felt refreshed; she could tell that someone had made sure she was clean. Suddenly, the cold sting of a needle pierced her left arm. She was conscious enough to realize that she was strapped down to this table, unable to move her hands and feet, and in her mouth was the same gag that made it impossible for her to scream for help hours prior.

"Hold still!" a voice commanded.

It was the man with the red face mask, although now, he no longer wore the rubber smock or face shield. He was standing beside her in a completely white, satin, one-piece uniform, and the red-silk face mask that only showed his cold brown eyes, which were now covered by plastic safety glasses. He finished inserting the IV drip in her arm and secured the needle with a thin plastic bandage.

Waves of panic started to grip her. "What's going on?" she wondered. "Why am I held down? Where am I? Is this a hospital?"

All of the thoughts ran through her mind at once, but it was the first thought that kept growing louder and louder: "What the fuck is going on? *What the fuck is going on?*"

The panic and fear was at such a point that she automatically started to cry, pull against the restraints, and scream. It was only a muffled scream, the gag made sure of that.

"Now, now…calm yourself," Brian said quietly.

She struggled more and more, finally gaining some slack with her right arm…It wasn't quite free, but if she kept pulling, straining at it, it just might loosen enough for her to pull her small hand through. The man had his back to her, measuring out a syringe with some bright-yellow liquid medication. She tugged twice more…she was almost free. With one final yell, she pulled her hand out of the cuff that held it to the table. As she reached up to undo the other cuff, Brian caught her arm, and in one smooth motion, slammed it back onto the table, holding it down with his much stronger right hand and using his left to stick the needle of the syringe into her neck. As he pushed down the plunger, she felt a coldness run through her veins. In a matter of heartbeats, her breathing slowed, she felt calm, and pleasure settled across her body. Brian reset the strap around her left wrist, cinching it even tighter. She never noticed. The pressure was there, but the pain wasn't.

Brian reopened the control screen and turned the music up louder. When he turned around to look at her, she was slowly undulating against the straps, but now in apparent pleasure, not defiance. Under the face mask, Brian smirked.

"She is quite the beautiful subject," he thought. "Thin and muscular with small, pert breasts and pointy, pink nipples, totally flawless except for a tattoo of a flower petal on her right hip."

"Too bad you don't have a dick," Brian said, "I might have enjoyed jerking your seed just to see if you're worthy of sparing."

*A rare chance*, Brian chuckled to himself.

He knew most men these days had the worst "swimmers" (sperm) if they could even produce any. The clones were all sterile by design, until The Council could get a good hold on total control of the lifespan of the populace, there was no way they would let clones beget clones. Human-natural born women were harvested then sterilized so young they never knew. In fact, in the education centers, it was taught that any kind of (menstrual) bleeding was the woman's (better told to them as 'girl's") body's way of rejecting something unnatural. What that was, didn't matter, it was left to be subjective on purpose just to leave the guilt of sin and pain to "obviously something they (the girl) had done wrong".

Brian never understood the want of inking perfectly intact flesh. Some of these people were so disgusting that he usually just took them for what they were: parts. But this one was different. As he stared at her lightly freckled face and blue eyes, he knew that this one, he was going to take for more. He put his hand on her cheek. She turned her head to him. Tears streamed from her eyes, but she was unable to move. He caressed her cheek for a moment, and then moved his hand down her body, first feeling her taut neck, then moving his hand across her chest and stopping to cup one small breast. With his gloved thumb and forefinger, he began to stroke, pinch, and flick her nipple. Despite her fear, her body betrayed her. Her nipples grew harder, and she let loose a slight moan that felt so distant, she wasn't sure it actually came from her.

Brian continued to move his hand downward, running his fingers in a circular pattern across her tight stomach. His fingers spent quite a bit of time, it seemed, rubbing and tracing the flower-petal tattoo just below her beltline. She no longer felt his hand until it was right on top of her vagina. With his index and middle fingers, he pushed open the folds of her labia, while pushing his middle finger inside her. A moan betrayed her once again, for although she was afraid, something in the drug was letting her body register nothing but pleasure. Brian heard the moan and saw her arch her pelvis as much as she could under the restraints. She was tight and wet, and he took this as his indication to go. He put another finger in, and while fucking her with his hand, he began to stroke her clit with his thumb. A few minutes of this finger play went on while Brian's middle finger pushed up to find her G-spot. With the movement of her hips, the shudder and moans of pleasure, it didn't take long for him to bring her to the edge. She felt the buildup, and just as the wave of euphoria from her orgasm took hold, she felt the cold sting of metal on her pelvis. She came. Waves of pleasure rippled through her, but that couldn't totally distract her from the pain of the scalpel pushing through her skin and cutting a square around her tattoo.

At this point, Brian had removed his fingers from her sex and was using both hands to cut out her tattoo.

With his right-gloved hand, covered in her cum, he packed gauze underneath the lifted flesh. He quickly used the scalpel to cut the tattoo away from her body in one solid piece. What was once the euphoria of her orgasm quickly gave way to the amplified pain of her skin being unceremoniously removed from her body.

Brian dropped the tattooed square of flesh in a jar of liquid on the tray. He sat the scalpel down next to it and picked up a preloaded syringe. He then pushed the needle of the syringe just below the skin in the area surrounding the open wound. The shock and horror fled from her face as the entire spot he was working on became completely numb. He put gauze on the wound and taped it down with bandages. The stress of the pleasure and pain left her drained, and Brian now figured it was time to get his.

He undid the ankle straps and linked them to the ones around her thighs with chain, pulling her down to the edge of the table and leaving her quivering vagina and ass hanging out. When he did this, the head/neck brace slid in unison. Brian ripped open the Velcro patch of his sterile suit and pulled out his large, engorged penis. She could not see what was happening; her head was still mounted to the table, and tears were streaming down her face. He held her legs apart as he pushed his cock into her asshole. The sudden pain caused her to scream, cry harder, and clench up. This seemed to turn him on as he let the head of his dick sit there and stretch her rectum. Brian then started to thrust his dick in and pull it slowly back, never pulling it completely out. After a few moments of the intense agony of this sodomy, he pushed in deeper than he had been and came inside her ass. He waited, pulled out, wiped his dick off with a green surgical towel, and stuffed it back inside his suit, closing the Velcro neatly and uniformly so all of the lines were aligned. A line of blood mixed with semen started to trickle out of her ass.

Sobbing profusely from the pain of the tattoo removal and the pain of having been anal-raped, her tears fogged her eyes to the layout of the room. Her nose was running, and her moans were no longer moans of pleasure but of pain—immense pain coursing throughout her body. She barely even noticed the pinprick against her neck, and in a few seconds, she passed out once more.

She woke up hanging on the wall of the cell. There were no lights. She could not see a door. She could only smell the moisture from the water running underneath the cage. She was still naked, and she realized that the gag was no longer in her mouth. Her arms, legs, and neck were still bound, but the straps that normally ran around her waist and chest now spanned her shoulders and hips. A sudden twinge of pain made her realize why: across her waist where the previous strap had been was the bandaged wound where the masked man had removed her tattoo. But new, and even worse, was the bandage that covered her breasts. Stains of blood seeped through the gauze, and she felt an unfathomable sharp pain where her nipples—"Oh, my God!" she thought. Tears started streaming down her face again. "They're gone!"

"You took my nipples, you sick fuck!" she yelled.

Then she screamed as loud as she could manage. IV bags providing nourishment, blood, saline, and just a small bit of morphine (not enough to kill the pain, but enough to prevent her from going into shock) hung just out of reach…not that she could get to them with her arms bolted down.

"Fucker! Motherfucker! Ahhhhhh!" she screamed.

A stream of urine flowed down her leg and pooled in the water on the floor, before the current pushed it into the drains beneath her feet. The eyeless face of her bulked companion in the corner just glared mockingly, unable to express any more than whatever she imagined he...it...was thinking. It was then that she noticed that, despite its penis still being attached, any other suggestion of its sex was...wait... she could see closer... the penis wasn't, it didn't belong to this poor victim. It was *sutured* on. Whether this was a man or woman before, no one would ever know without a proper autopsy, but it had been morbidly "re-fashioned" to what that butcher wanted to make it. This was not the natural remains of a human man, but the discards of a failed art project. Her fear and anger poured out of her in screams she didn't know she could produce.

The screams were of no use however, for out in the basement, the lights had been restored; Brian had showered in the washroom and put his regular attire back on. The autopsy table had been sprayed down. In fact, everything seemed nice, clean, and reorganized. He placed his sterile suit, gloves, and boots in a plastic bag and pushed it through a white plastic door to an incinerator. Brian was meticulous about not leaving any evidence—not that anyone knew he was down there. He began to hear screams coming from the cage room and turned his music up to drown them out.

He then walked over to the steel door leading to the stairway. Next to it was another steel door, this one only having a numerical keypad. He typed the code 7734, and the door slid open. Once inside the room, he pushed a button to close the steel door. In this room was his private office and library. Thousands upon thousands of tomes: textbooks, reference books, medical journals, biographies of famous celebrities, and most noticeably, a large selection of books on the lives and infamy of the turn-of-the-millennium killers.

Among the gold-laced, red-ochre-framed documents on the walls were awards to Dr. Brian Douglas for his contributions to medicine and pharmacology. Brian sat down in his green-leather executive desk chair. His desk was clean and organized; nothing seemed to be out of place except the three clear jars sitting at the edge of the desk, two of which contained his "play-friend's" nipples, which he'd placed on spikes to prevent them from moving in the clear, preservative solution. In the third, her flower-petal tattoo sat in the same solution, but steel clasps on all four corners held the flesh taut.

Brian sighed and reached into the cigar humidor on his desk. He pulled out a fat, good-smelling Cohiba cigar. Opening the top drawer of his desk, he pulled out a cigar cutter and a lighter. He cut the end off the cigar and proceeded to light it. He leaned back in his chair. The drag of cigar smoke calmed his nerves, and he put his feet up and listened to the mixture of Bach and his victim's screams in a glorious chorus.

# FOUR

"Have your men finished yet, Detective?" Rikoh was stern and cold, not showing any regard for the body in the glass case before him.

A woman's body, it had been carefully dissected piece by piece until only major organs remained. However, the organs were not entirely inside the case of skin, as nature intended. Every piece was put on display, and they were held together by a metallic frame to show an exploded view of her body. Skin and muscle were still intact on her limbs, but each piece of her body was disconnected from its adjacent parts. Her vital organs—heart, liver, and brain—were thrust directly out from where they were supposed to be and attached to the torso and head by metal poles. Her face and the top of her head were missing, leaving this former person, or rather parts of a person, looking like a full-size mock-up in an anatomical textbook.

"What's ya got, Reeves?" Detective Riley asked the man in the blue LAB jacket.

"The room has been mapped, and the blood, tested. There's a hole in the bottom of the enclosure that probably caused the excess blood to leak, but judging by the degree of oxidation, we're putting the blood at over two weeks old. Of course, we'll have to get it back to the morgue to find out who these parts belong to, but they seem asymmetrical. Our theory is that this...display...was put here last night, but the parts inside are rejects. Another of those flesh freaks," the man in the blue LAB jacket said.

"Fuckin' crazy assholes," Riley said. "Bitch is probably walking around town with state-of-the art limbs."

Simon couldn't help himself; he had to chime in. "That's assuming these are different parts from different people..."

Riley glared at Simon.

"Don't forget your place, Sy...You's retired now, right?"

Simon knew better than to push the argument. He bit his tongue.

"Yeah, sorry. Old habits, you know..."

Riley grunted. Then he walked over and, in a sudden sympathetic move, put his hand on Simon's shoulder. He spoke in a low voice so only Simon could hear.

"Heya listen, Sy. I knows you's trying ta help, but anybody else catches windy wind that you's down here, and it's both our asses, if ya know what I mean..."

Simon nodded. He followed Rikoh past the rear of the case and looked back.

"Who put this here? Why?" he thought.

Rikoh's missing "objet d'art" seemed much more interesting. He dared not say anything, but through a slight strain of his eye, he made sure that his contacts recorded what he saw.

"This way, Mr. Topaz." Rikoh seemed annoyed by Simon's interest in the body.

"Yes, of course," said Simon.

He was here, after all, only to find the missing scissors.

Rikoh led him around the corner of the office into a separate room with a large metal door. On the wall was a screen that Rikoh approached, bowed down before, and stared into. All at once, the door opened.

"Retinal scanner?" asked Simon.

"Top-of-the-line security measures," replied Rikoh.

They walked inside a decently sized room with metal shelves lining the walls. Covered plastic boxes took up most of the floor space and filled most of the shelves. Rikoh walked over to a particular box on a middle shelf, just under chest-height, and put his thumb on the front, next to a label that merely said "BLITHE." There was a mechanical whir as tumblers and motors released the lid of the box.

"Top of the line," he stated matter-of-factly.

"So," Simon asked, "who, then, all has access to the room and artifacts?"

"Only myself and Ms. Sanchez can enter the room. All the boxes that pertain to my exhibit can only be opened by me."

"Do you have any idea as to who may have been in here and taken the item?"

"Mr. Topaz, that is why I hired you," Rikoh stated flatly.

"No one should have been able to get into this room or to know to take the one true artifact in the room, let alone open the correct box."

"And you didn't take it yourself...maybe by mistake?"

"To what purpose?" Rikoh was irritated by the insinuation.

"Who knows? Insurance money? Personal collection?"

"No, Mr. Topaz. I would not be paying your fee and expenses just to waste our time."

"Well, I have to ask," said Simon.

The stress meter in his contacts was reading low. Either Rikoh was telling the truth, or he had a lot of practice at being a good liar.

Simon walked over to look in the box. Inside were some more photos of the Blithe family in happier times. Next to the stack of photos was a rectangular foam cutout where the box with the real scissors should have sat.

"Do you mind if I look at these?" asked Simon, indicating the photos.

"No, but please wear these." Rikoh produced two pairs of white silk gloves for Simon and himself. "And I need not remind you that these are priceless artifacts."

"You need not," Simon said, mocking Rikoh's tone. With his newly gloved hands, Simon picked up the photos and started sorting through them.

The Blithe family seemed like a typical American family. He remembered learning of their story years ago when studying criminal justice. The first photo Simon came across showed them at what seemed to be a picnic or family outing. Jeremy and

Martha Blithe, ever the proud parents, had beaming smiles on their faces. In Martha's arms lay little Jenny, only six months old at the time of the picture. Standing in front were three kids: Renee, who was seven, and another girl whose name Simon couldn't recall, who was about ten years old. On the end was their infamous older brother, Brian Blithe, fifteen years old and playing the role of angsty teenager to the hilt. While everyone else in the picture had a neat, groomed appearance—a masquerade of the ideal family—only Brian showed his true colors. His black, straight, shoulder-length hair covered one side of his face, and he had a scowl to match. The date stamped in the corner was October 10, 2018.

Simon made sure to take a solid image capture of what he was seeing with his contacts, knowing that this may be the only time that he would have access to these pictures. He shuffled through the other pictures, which were all pretty much the same. They showed the family or members of the family in various "ideal" family-time merriment. There was nothing salacious or intriguing about any of the photos, and had he not known the history, he would have thought these pictures were ordinary family photos. Something in his gut told Simon that something was amiss, however, and when he had time away from Rikoh's hovering and the pressure of finding a golden clue at the scene of the crime, he would have to study his copies of the photos in detail. For now, he felt comfortable putting the originals back in the box.

Simon heard a noise outside the room and looked out the door. The police had been efficient in covering the display case of body parts with a black cloth and in sealing the leaking hole. Some men were using pneumatic lifters to put rolling dollies underneath the case, while others were cleaning up what was left of the blood on the floor. Within five minutes, the case was being rolled out of the gallery, and no visible trace of its temporary residence remained.

"Any conclusions, Mr. Topaz?" asked Rikoh. His tone suggested his irritation. Simon was spending too much time worrying about what the police were doing and not nearly enough time on the job he was being paid to do.

"Is there security footage?" Simon asked.

"Not in this area of the building, but MELaNIE monitors for any motion, heat, break-ins, and so on."

"Who's MELaNie?"

Rikoh pulled a small controller from his pocket and touched the tops of three buttons.

"MEL, acknowledge," Rikoh said into the air.

"ACKNOWLEGDED. GOOD MORNING, MR. RIKOH."

Rikoh, having put the fob back in his pocket, looked at Simon.

"MELaNIE is the building's support and security system. We had it...her...upgraded to the highest end before I would allow the exhibition to take place. Ms. Sanchez and I are the only voices authorized to operate her, and only one person, a Miss Christine Danam, the programmer, can make any changes to her programming."

"Can I meet with Miss Danam?"

"I'm sure that can be arranged. But I should tell you that she has the highest-level security clearance, and she has programmed systems for the elite, including our exalted leader himself. Her record is quite impeccable."

"I don't doubt it," said Simon. "Still, it would be good to know what possible ways someone could place a giant case of FleshArt in an auspicious gallery late at night and steal an artifact of no commercial value, while avoiding a top-level security system to which, you said yourself, only three people have access."

Rikoh managed to crack a smile; he'd finally heard something that pleased him. "So you *will* find my artifact then, Mr. Topaz?" he asked, already knowing the answer.

"I won't promise you I'll find it, but I *can* guarantee that you'll know who stole it and where it is."

"Indeed," Rikoh said, satisfied. "How can I best assist you?"

"I'll need access to MELaNIE's records, any recordings, measurements…any data she recorded last night. I'd also like to speak to Miss Sanchez and this Miss Danam. If you can set up meetings at my office later today, it would be best. Other than that, I'll report back to you any new developments I come across," Simon told Rikoh.

"Very well. I will get you a terminal set here in the office to converse with MEL, but I'm not sure what you're hoping to find. I've personally been through the records. I will contact you later regarding misses Sanchez and Danam. Now, if you'll excuse me, I'll have someone in shortly to let you talk to MEL."

Rikoh turned and started to walk out the door when Simon suddenly spoke.

"Mr. Rikoh, before you go, I *do* have one question to ask. How exactly did you realize the artifact was missing?"

Rikoh did not turn around; he stopped and spoke over his shoulder. "I've had quite a bit of interest, recently, from people inquiring about this piece...more than others...more than usual. When I heard what happened and came by last night, I had..." He paused. "I had a feeling. I inspected everything and found only the scissors to be missing. Will that be all, Mr. Topaz?"

"Yes, sir. Just curious," Simon answered.

As Rikoh walked away, Simon knew, through the stress meter in his contacts, that at least part of what Rikoh had just said was a blatant lie.

# FIVE

Just outside the looming security walls around the slums lay the skeletons of many abandoned factory buildings and warehouses. Mostly home to the rats and cockroaches, a lone warehouse had lights on and signs of human activity. The blue-and-gray-brick building had three large cargo roll-up doors and a two-space declined loading dock for large trucks to meet the level of the building. Large planks of wood that had been nailed there many years ago shuttered the front glass doors and windows. The one regular entry door was hidden by the overgrowth of plants, which had decided to take the land back for themselves after so many years of human neglect. The vegetation had been parted in such a way that while the door remained hidden, those who knew the path would have no trouble finding it.

The interior of the building was quite the opposite in appearance. In the central warehouse sat a stage six feet off the ground. The stage, walls, floor, and even the stairs to the side of the stage had been painted black. Around the stage stood a black trussing grid of aluminum and steel. Hidden in the trussing were robotic lighting fixtures, speakers, and a system of pulleys and motors whose wires, ropes, and chains ended with either a hook or a shackle.

In the front of the building, separated from the floor-show area by black-painted and soundproof walls, stood the gallery. Soft jazz music floated down from the ceiling speakers in the gallery. The walls were stained a dark purple, and large, blue, velour drapes hung down between the exhibits. Only Andre knew the exact count, but there were more than two hundred pieces being shown. Some were paintings done in bodily fluids: blood, saliva, semen, and feces. Others were stand-alone glass and acrylic cases, each containing a single body part encased in resin: an ear, an eye, an arm, or a leg. At one end of the gallery was Andre's pride in the collection: surgical instruments and machines dating back to the dawn of modern medicine.

Beyond the expansive gallery was a hidden stairwell. On the second story of the building, adorned with candelabras and gothic sconces that bathed the room in a warm glow, was Andre's office. Outside the office stood a large freezer door with a spray-painted sign that read "morgue."

Andre was kneeling on a cushion in the middle of the floor, his back to the door, meditating. He heard her footsteps as she came up the stairs. He knew the sound of his sister's gait. Besides, she was the only person he was expecting. With his eyes still closed and wisps of Frankincense trailing though the cracked beams of sunlight, he spoke into the air.

"Open locks 143 and 144."

The faint sound of tumblers disengaging and the mild crackle of the static-electric field in front of his office door disappearing were signs enough of that his order had been heard and obeyed. Not seconds later, he heard a faint knock on the door.

"Come in," Andre said in a low voice.

"Andre, I brought you that new candidate, as I promised. He's waiting down in the parlor." The voice was that of Christine, Andre's sister.

"Very good," said Andre as he opened his gray eyes and stood.

He was wearing slacks and a flowing, white, twill shirt that hung loosely on his wiry frame. He reached down to the desk for his black, horn-rimmed glasses and pushed them onto his worn, pockmarked face. He ran his thin, bony hands through his long, brown hair, pulling it back into a ponytail. He looked at Chris.

Although she was only thirty-two (twenty years his junior) and only his half sister, he was still amazed at how youthful and beautiful she looked. She, too, had a thin frame, but it was muscular, with wide, strong hips that, as she would say, were her greatest "ASS-et." Straight, purple hair framed her face. Her petite nose and pronounced chin were complemented well by her large, hazel eyes. A small diamond stud pierced her lower lip, and she had a matching one in her right nostril. Her thin eyebrows were brunette and revealed the natural color of her hair. She was wearing a black T-shirt, jeans, and black-leather combat boots laced to the top but not tied. Her right arm was entirely tattooed from her wrist to her shoulder; her left had just two tattoos: a large design on the inside of her upper arm and a flower on her wrist. Peeking out from the neck of her shirt were the points of different-sized stars that made a tattooed necklace.

"Is it too soon?" she asked Andre.

Andre smiled. "Never," he said, and picked up a green ampul from his desk.

He walked over to Chris, took her hand in his, palm up, and set the ampul in it. He gently closed her hand around the ampul and kissed her on the forehead.

"It's for the pain," she said as her eyes welled up with tears. "I…"

Andre put his finger to her lips as he whispered, "Shh…I know. I know."

A single tear managed to escape her eye and run down her cheek before she wiped her eyes dry with the back of her hand.

"Come now," said Andre as he gently put his hands on Chris's shoulders.

He smiled. "Let's attend to our guest."

She nodded. Andre walked to the door and took a purple-and-black satin robe from a hook on the wall. Behind him, he could hear Christine pull the shiny metal tube from the front pocket of her jeans. She put the ampul in the end of the tube and watched as the meter, which read nearly empty, began to recharge. The meter level rose as the liquid in the ampul was sucked into the tube. Andre put on his robe and tied it in the front. He placed his feet in a pair of purple-and-black slippers. At the same time, Christine pulled down the neck of her shirt and placed the end of the silver cylinder in the middle of a small star tattoo near her jugular vein. She pressed an indented button and felt a prick as the needle pierced her skin. Within a heartbeat, her pupils widened, and she felt relaxed but energized. Someone once named it the "IT effect." Chris couldn't care less what it was called; she loved the rush of pleasure and euphoria she felt as her skin went numb. IT caressed her body in a warm glow. She put the pen back in her pocket and walked over to Andre, beaming.

"Better?" he asked with a laugh.

"Much," she said as they walked downstairs together.

\*\*\*

"Welcome, friend. How may I be of service?"

Andre always waxed poetic when speaking with a client. The man he was facing was dressed as well as he could, but the suit was tattered and wrinkled. He wore an eye patch.

"I thank ya kindly for seeing me, Mr...."

"Andre."

"Mr. Andre."

"No. Please, friend, just call me Andre."

The poor man continued: "Well, Andre...I done lost my eye in an accident some years ago and...well, truth be told, when I heard that I could make enough money being in your... um... performance... to buy a new eye, well, sir—"

Andre finished the sentence for him. "You had no other choice than to come see me. And indeed, it was the right choice..."

The man was slow to realize that Andre was asking for his name.

"Oh, um, Bob...sir."

"Yes, Robert, as I was saying, you did not have much alternative, so I imagine. Well, fate has brought us together, Robert. Not only can I pay you well for your performance, but we also have the finest medical staff on hand to attach your new eye, so you will see with the utmost clarity."

"Well, gee, Andre, sir, that sounds great!"

The poor man was excited and rushed over to shake Andre's hand. Andre put a hand on the poor man's back and gently guided him toward the stairwell.

"I'm glad you're on board, Robert. Let's sort out the details in my office."

As they left, Chris chuckled at the poor man's demeanor. She suddenly felt her phone begin to vibrate in her pocket. She looked at the screen. It simply said, "Call Incoming: R." She knew who that was.

"Why would he want to talk to me now?" she wondered.

She walked into the gallery, where she would not be heard. Rikoh's face appeared on the small screen. He was calm and collected, as usual.

"Greetings, Chris. I have a request," he said.

"Never one to beat around the bush," she thought.

"Yes, Rikoh. How can I help you?"

"The detective I hired, a Mr. Simon Topaz, wants to speak with you. I will let him know you'll be by his office tomorrow afternoon. I am sending you the address now."

"Why does he need to meet with me?" she asked.

"Since you programmed MELaNIE, he would

like to discuss her security features. But there's more."

"Yes?"

"Mr. Topaz has intraspectral lenses. They're carefully hidden, but I did notice them. I need you to break into his apartment tonight and erase any data he may have recorded of me and/or anything to do with a Blithe family once we were inside the vault. He is a heavy IT user, so I don't suspect you should have too much trouble," Rikoh said, grinning.

"No problem. I'm on it. Tell him I'll meet him at 4:00 p.m. tomorrow afternoon."

"Thank you, my dearest Chris. Ciao."

Rikoh's face disappeared from the screen. If she hadn't been feeling so good from the hit of IT, she would have been shaking. Rikoh was always leering and lurking after her; it made her more than uncomfortable. She walked back into the parlor just in time to see Andre and Bob coming into the room.

"So, we're agreed, Robert," said Andre. "You know the risks, but better, the rewards. I'll see you again tomorrow night. Christine will show you out."

Bob was elated.

Chris decided not to tell her brother about the caller. "After all, he would just worry," she thought.

"Tomorrow night, then?" asked Bob.

"Tomorrow night," Andre and Chris said in unison.

Bob giggled. "Tomorrow night," he muttered to himself.

Andre smiled and slowly waved as Chris led Bob out of the building.

She chuckled. "Poor fool thinks he is excited

now," she thought. "Wait until tomorrow."

# SIX

It was approaching noon, and Simon was getting tired, looking at the hours of monotonous camera footage he'd requested. He had spent most of the morning watching over twenty camera angles from inside the gallery and out. Sipping a cup of coffee, he tried to concentrate on the images as they fluttered by, but between the tedium of watching nothing happen and the cacophony of police forensics investigators just outside the small office Rikoh had set up for him, his interest in the footage was waning, and distractions were growing.

"MEL, roll security footage from 6:00 p.m. last night to present from camera 17, twenty x speed."

Again, he saw the same images from a different angle; and again, nothing unusual showed up. The fact that there was nothing unusual was unusual in itself. Simon couldn't understand it. He'd viewed more than half of the camera footage. It was as if a ghost had come in the night before.

He had seen objective angles of the office area, the entrance to the vault, and the front door of the gallery, but nothing happened from the time Rikoh left at 7:14:32 to the sudden appearance of the cased body at midnight sharp. In many places, Simon had paused and zoomed in on the image, looking for discrepancies between frames, but nothing. The box isn't there, and then it suddenly is. The pulsing in his head was starting to become a throb as his patience wore thin.

Camera 17 was aimed at the office door, from the inside and apparently from the ceiling. Simon paused and toggled the frames with a handheld controller. He let it playback and still, nothing. Nothing was out of place or gave any indication that the footage might have been tampered with. The time coding was correct, and the box, again, just appeared.

Simon sighed and began to drink his coffee again, only this time he noticed a sharp burn in his mouth. He knew what it meant; he was coming down and would start to have delirium tremens soon. If he waited too long, not only would the pain be amplified, but the hallucinations would start kicking in, and for Simon, being able to suppress recent memories was all that kept him from going mad.

He got up from his chair and walked down the hall to the washroom. Two other men, cops, were already in the room. He waited for them to leave before he pulled the injection pen from his pocket. His hands were already starting to shake. He fumbled as best he could with the dial, this time turning it to a five-microgram dose. Everything in his body was starting to feel alive again, and not in a pleasant way. He opened the buttons on his shirt and put the tip of the pen on the small $X$ tattooed on his chest, directly over his heart. Pressing the button, he felt the sudden pierce of the needle, and the door opened on him. A police officer whom he didn't know had almost caught him dosing. Simon was able to discreetly hide the pen in his palm and slip it back into his pants pocket with one hand, while using his other to wipe imaginary crumbs off his shirt.

"I think I might need a bib," he quipped.

The man was not at all interested, which was exactly what Simon had hoped for. He felt the rush of the IT soothe and numb his body once again. At the same time, it made him hyperfocused. He buttoned up his shirt and left the washroom, no one the wiser. Or so he thought.

***

From an office across town, Rikoh was watching Simon's every move. Standing behind Rikoh was Dr. Brian Douglas. Brian looked at Rikoh, smiled, and nodded, when there was a knock at the door.

"Yes?" Brian asked.

A female voice answered his query. "Doctor, Robert Holmsted is ready for you."

"Thank you. I'll be right in."

Brian looked down at Rikoh. "I'll be back shortly. Our newest candidate is here."

Brian pointed to Simon's figure on the screen. "Make sure he's our guest tomorrow night. I don't want him to miss the show." He patted Rikoh on the shoulder, and then turned and walked out of the room.

Rikoh turned on the videophone on his desk and pushed the button labeled Recent Calls. Topaz was listed third. He pushed the Audio Only and Call buttons in sequence. He could see Simon sitting at the screen, but Simon didn't know that. Simon looked at his phone, which flashed with the message, Incoming Call—Rikoh.

"This is Simon."

"Yes, Mr. Topaz, I wanted to inform you that misses Sanchez and Danam will be at your office at 1:00 p.m. and 4:00 p.m. tomorrow, respectively," said Rikoh.

"Great. Thank you, Rikoh."

"Any information yet, Mr. Topaz?" Rikoh asked.

"Nothing so far. I'm still sorting through the video footage from last night, but so far, it doesn't make much sense—things aren't there, and then suddenly, they are. Are you sure no one else had access to this footage?"

"Only myself, Miss Sanchez, and Miss Danam have access. No one else."

"Are you sure? Maybe a vendor or contractor? What about anyone hacking the system?"

"Quite impossible. The time it would take to break into the system and edit the footage from twenty different cameras…they would still be doing it now, as we speak."

Rikoh was telling the truth, or at least what he believed to be true. Simon could tell that by the audio analyzer in his contact lenses. It detected no stress in his voice. "Then that's all I have for you now, Mr. Rikoh," said Simon.

When he realized that Rikoh, seemingly placated, had ended the connection, Simon just shook his head. "Asshole," he thought.

In another quiet room, behind another quiet screen, Christine Danam was just finishing editing last night's security camera footage from the Manna

Gallery. Per Rikoh's instruction, she'd erased the footage showing Andre and Rikoh pulling up to the gallery last night in a large cargo van, removing a large box covered with a black drape from the truck, rolling it into the building, setting the box in the office of one Miss Rosalee Sanchez, and removing the drape to reveal a grotesque display of body parts. She was not aware that she was only an hour ahead of Simon, who was watching the footage of last night's events, or even that Simon had been painstakingly trudging through her handiwork all morning. Neither did she know that Rikoh was watching *her*.

Through the window, the sun began waning. Simon wiped his eyes and then looked at his watch. It was now past four in the afternoon, and he'd just finished watching the last of the security footage. Nothing. He'd figured that something, no matter how small, would seem out of place or leave a clue. All twenty cameras showed the same thing, just from different angles.

"I'm wasting too much time on each of these," he thought. "They're all the same…all of them…all…"

The word "all" kept nagging him. He decided to try a different tactic.

"MEL, show me the footage from all of the cameras on screen, split view, same time frame."

As he watched the videos playback in synchronicity, he finally saw it. This was what he was looking for. Toggling the paused image back and forth, frame by frame, just after the time code read 12:00.00, he saw the glitch. Of all the views of Miss Sanchez's office and the horrible case placed there, four showed the floor well enough to see the pool of blood that had leaked out over the night. But footage from one camera, camera 18, was different. The pool was much larger on camera 18 than from any other view.

"MEL, isolate cameras 6, 12, 17, and 18, on a split screen."

The four camera angles all zoomed in, splitting the screen into quadrants. He let the video play in real time. The pool of blood that ran to the office door was noticeably bigger in the footage from camera 18. Using different items in the office as reference points, he estimated that the blood spot in the camera 18 footage advanced three to four inches closer to the door in the same period. Simon felt both elated and disappointed. Here was evidence that the footage *had* been tampered with, but he still had nothing to go on.

"Only myself, Miss Sanchez, and Miss Danam have access. No one else." Simon turned Rikoh's statement over in his mind. "Of those three," Simon thought, "only one has the apparent skill to edit this. I need to find Christine Danam."

***

Chris had just opened the door to her own apartment. Nino, her kitten, was right at her legs to meet her, almost tripping her.

"Hey, sweetie," she said to the cat. "Mommy's home."

A mew and purr came from the kitten, which she picked up carefully, kissing it on the head. Holding the kitten with one hand, she closed and bolted the front door with the other. She sat Nino on the table, opened a fresh can of cat food, and put it in front of the kitten. Nino started eating, and so did Chris, cutting slices of an apple with a small paring knife. She looked at the clock. It was 5:45 p.m. Chris knew that she had to break into this Simon's place later that night, but now, it was time to relax after a frantic few days of work.

She loosened the laces on her boots and kicked them off as she plopped down on her couch. Her toenails were painted purple. A giant lotus flower tattoo covered the top of one foot. On the other foot were Latin words that she didn't know the meaning of. She turned on her holoscreen and started cycling through channels. Images of people engaged in concerts or some sporting contest appeared in her living room. The next channel was a newscast. She left it there and got off the couch to take a shower. She took off her clothes in the bathroom, never aware that Rikoh was watching her every move.

\*\*\*

Rikoh was still in an office at Brian's practice, watching all of the players in his game. And of all the players, he liked Chris the best. Rikoh got up from his chair and checked the lock on the door. It was secure. Watching Chris get undressed had made him feel…amorous. He sat back down, aware of the hard-on in his pants. He zoomed in on Chris, taking still shots for his pleasure later. Rikoh started to stroke his dick from outside his pants; his role as a passive observer would have to work… for the moment.

He focused the hidden camera on her hairless crotch. A tattoo of a multicolored butterfly stretched across her pubic area. He zoomed the camera out and then back in on her tits; both of her large, dark-red nipples were pierced with studs, and he could clearly see the detail of art on her torso. A large snake tattoo wound around her side and coiled at her belly button. On the other side of her stomach was a cartoon ghost from a popular children's show. Just seeing her standing there nude, setting the temperature of the shower, and checking the water, made his hand move faster along his prick.

Rikoh stared at her face, a face he'd wanted for years. Ever since he first met her, he wanted to do horrible things to her beautiful, innocent face. He worked for Brian, and she was some whore filth that captured his eye when Brian found Andre.

"A beautiful flower among the shit, rust, and decay of the common people," he thought.

She was smart; Rikoh could tell that from the very beginning. And she knew ways of using her femininity to guarantee her survival among the wretched. He had worked himself into such a frenzy of wanting, desiring, fantasizing about her that he was caught off guard by his need to cum. Just as he was exploding inside the pant leg of his neat suit, the videophone suddenly came to life. It was Simon, interrupting his moment of pleasure with the desire to speak business.

"Fuck!" Rikoh thought. "Fuck, fuck him, fuck him...fucking junkies...I'll make them all pay! Simon for his nuisance, and Chris for daring to seduce me, the foul, fucking temptress!"

His hand sticky with the ejaculate that was

now soaking through the fabric of his pants, he pressed the answer button, making sure the video was muted.

"Yes?" he asked angrily.

"Umm…yeah. Mr. Rikoh, it's Simon. I just wanted to let you know that I've finished what I can do for now at the gallery. I'll be heading back to my office shortly."

"Yes. Fine. Any news?" Rikoh asked.

"I found an anomaly in the footage. It's probably just a glitch, but it is imperative that I speak to Miss Danam."

"An anomaly?" Rikoh wondered. "Did that fucking whore sell me out? Or is she dumber and sloppier than I gave her credit for? No matter," he assured himself. "The plan is now in motion, and nothing can change it."

"Yes. Yes. She will be at your office tomorrow, promptly at four, as promised," said Rikoh. "Good day, Mr. Topaz."

He ended the call and went into an adjacent washroom to change his pants and clean himself from the mess Christine caused. When he returned, she was already out of the shower, drying off. A towel was wrapped around her torso. Rikoh grew angry thinking of the way she exploited him, even turning his own body and carnal impulses against his will. As he watched Chris walk out of the bathroom, his fist flew into the monitor, causing the image to go dead and the screen to fracture like a giant spider web.

"Fucking junkies," thought Rikoh. "They will both pay dearly."

***

In her apartment, Chris had just put on an all-black outfit, when the videophone light showed a waiting message. It was from Rikoh.

"Chris, we may have a problem. Simon said he found something but wouldn't go into detail. Be on your guard."

She knew she'd been careful erasing the footage and wondered if maybe Simon was bluffing. "Either way," she thought. "Time to meet the infamous Simon Topaz."

# SEVEN

Simon walked into his apartment; he was ready to download the day's events and sort through the notes he had taken. He put on an old album of jazz music. Even with today's sophisticated crystal storage units and laser audio players, Simon preferred the nostalgia of an old plastic disk. Perhaps it sounded awful in comparison, but there was a warmth, a presence he felt in the music that wasn't otherwise there. These discs, called record albums, had been handed down in his family for four hundred years. They dated back to the twentieth century. He kept the records in a sealed, nitrogen-filled container; machines took care of the delicate work of handling the discs. The record player was similar to another machine from that era in his collection—something called a "jukebox" that was a storage unit, a player, and an amplifier all in one case. He wasn't entirely familiar with the music playing now—the label said Miles Davis. All he knew was that it soothed him. Simon turned down the lights to a soft glow and took out his contacts, putting them in a case that not only protected them but also read the information he'd collected during the day. He was tired, but he still had quite a bit of work to do.

Simon took a shower and dressed, this time in dark-blue silk pajama pants. Standing in the living room, he opened the drawer of a large wooden bureau, and inside sat another injection pen. It was similar to the one he left in his pants pocket, but it had a large threaded port on the side opposite the needle. A row of small glass vials, each with a threaded neck, sat next to the pen. Each vial was filled with the green, glowing liquid IT, but in different hues. The label on each bottle showed that it was hospital stock, which cost quite a bit extra, but he didn't mind. The street-grade IT was okay to get him through the day, but this was pharmaceutical-grade IT, ten to twenty times the strength of the street stuff. That amount of IT could easily kill or worse. Worse was just enough IT to fry the synapses in a human brain but leave the body's primary autonomous systems (organ control, respiration, etc.) alone, sending the user into a permanent state of paralysis. The dissociative effect made the body useless other than to trap the personality—some said the soul—of a person inside his or her own body.

When IT first appeared in research labs, it was hailed as the ideal surgical anesthetic—that was, until clinical trials on humans showed that even though the body was numb and sedated, the patient was not only conscious but hyperaware during the entire procedure. The mental trauma of being awake but unable to communicate while their innards were cut and removed, bones were broken, and muscles were torn apart was too much for the early patients. The use of IT for recreation didn't take hold until fifty years ago.

That was when Leader announced a new

program to promote the repopulating of New Eden by taking the burdens of childbirth and child-rearing away from everyday people and mechanizing them. Having a child was not illegal, but for many different reasons, fertility was difficult, and so most of today's population had been born to anonymous parents in places called "Genesis Centers." Only the people who worked in those centers, whose function was to be "birthers," and some of the people who ran the program at the government level knew in detail what happened in them. Simon was born a natural baby, not in a Genesis Center, but he never knew his parents. He was told they perished in a car accident days after he was born. Simon was raised and educated alongside the "pureborn" children. He was not genetically refined, however, which was good in some ways and bad in others. Good in the sense that he was not inclined to fit his work, that he was capable of more free thought than they were. Bad because in times such as this—and when he was hospitalized, recovering from the trauma the Sindel Cartel inflicted—his body did not react the same way to many medications, including IT, that a pureborn's did.

He pulled out the vial of concentrated IT and screwed the injection pen onto it. Soft jazz music was playing in the background when he sat down in the oversized recliner and put the pen to his neck. Pushing the button, he felt a quick sting and closed his eyes. He was ready to disappear from time and space, separating his body and mind. His body relaxed and his breathing slowing to a deep crawl, Simon was ready to fall into the arms of an IT dream.

\*\*\*

Simon's eyes were closed, but he felt as though he could see through them. Everything in the room before him was the same until the edges of the room started to break apart in swirls of geometric shapes that changed into a rainbow of colors. He could feel his heart beating in synchronization with the movement of purple, blue, and green clouds. As the clouds evaporated, he was left in the dark. He was calm and comfortable, but the feeling of nothingness surrounded him. The black void pulled his essence from his body, and he was left as an observer. He remembered scenes from throughout his life: a party Anne threw for his thirtieth birthday, joking around with Riley at the station, good times with friends, laughs…so many laughs. He saw a picnic he went on with Anne once. It was their second date, and he was so nervous that he spilled wine down the front of his shirt. She laughed at him.

"Don't look," he'd said, teasing, as she sat in the sun, smiling, laughing.

"Why not? You're not shy, are you?" Anne had asked him.

"Yes," he'd said, laughing. "Very!"

He was wearing an undershirt, but she had done as he asked and turned her head away. When she turned back to him, her face was no longer her face; it was that of another woman. The face was beautiful, and the woman spoke to him in Anne's voice.

"I think I can get used to this," she said, but she was not Anne anymore.

He didn't know this new woman, but the scene was already playing back the way it happened. He leaned in to kiss her...Anne...whoever this was, and as their lips met, he felt the warmth of love pass over him live waves of sunlight. The sky kept changing colors, and as her kissed her deeper, more passionately, her hair started to turn from Anne's straight, long, blond hair, to shoulder-length brown hair with bangs that ended just above her eyebrows. He stared into her eyes, but he no longer knew whose eyes they were...and when she blinked, her eyes were no longer there, only black and bloodstained orbits remained. The sky turned red and dark as he returned to the blackness of the void. Simon wasn't afraid of the things he was seeing, but he felt cold.

Suddenly, he saw an empty abandoned house in the middle of the desert, and the sun turned everything he looked at into shades of black and white. He walked into the house and found himself in perdition, at the gates of a giant castle. A moat of fire and lava burned all around him in a brilliant white light, but all he could feel was the cold emptiness of where he was standing. Demons crawled around the rocks, ignoring Simon, carrying different dismembered body parts with them. One demon had the face of Rikoh, and Simon watched as the demon began eating the entrails of a mouthless young woman. She was still alive and being disemboweled, and as she thrashed helplessly, Simon felt the arms of a woman wrap around him and pull him back into the void.

He felt comfortable, safe, and secure in her arms. She kissed his neck as he turned, and again he saw the mystery woman. They kissed in a passionate embrace, but Simon could see Anne, in a white gown, standing there watching them. Anne was smiling, and she turned and walked away in slow motion. Simon wanted to yell for her, but he couldn't. He was lying on the ground, alone in a green field. He heard Anne's voice in his head.

"It's time to go," she said.

As the warm sun passed overhead into night, he entered the void one last time. This time, however, the blackness did not carry him. It began to form colors and objects around him. He felt loved and confident, but seeing the objects take shape into his living room, he knew that his dream was over. It was time to wake up.

***

Simon opened his eyes slowly. By the clock, he could tell that he had been passed out for about four hours. He was awake and alert, but his body was still relaxed and warm. The feeling was the closest to "good" he experienced anymore. He slowly got out of the chair and dragged himself into the bedroom, lurching onto the bed on top of the sheets.

"Lights," he managed to say, and though the word was slurred, it was enough. The dull warm glow of the room faded into blackness.

Simon closed his eyes for only a few minutes. He thought he heard something stirring in the next room, but he wasn't sure what it was. He put the sound off to his imagination, or maybe it was a residual effect of the IT trance. Simon felt himself start to drift off to sleep when he heard it again. The sound was quiet, but it was there—it almost sounded like…footsteps? Simon opened his eyes, and without moving his body, peered into the corridor. A person's shadow was cast on the floor, and Simon was very aware that he was not alone. "How the…" he wondered.

His apartment was thirteen floors up. There was no way to access it from the outside except the balcony, and even then, the security sensors should have triggered an alarm. Trying not to make any noise, Simon slid out of bed, carrying the small knife he kept underneath his pillow. He rushed up to the wall next to the door and put his back against it, so as not to be seen. Peering around the corner, he glimpsed a small figure dressed in black and wearing a black hood and mask. The person was small framed like a young boy, and he was looking for something, opening drawers quickly and stealthily. This wasn't just an average thief; this person had skills in being covert.

Simon slid his feet across the carpet to dampen the sound of his approach as he crept closer and closer. In three quick steps, Simon was immediately behind the figure, his arm locked around the intruder's waist and the knife at his throat.

"Lights!" he shouted.

The room lit up. The intruder, startled, froze and tensed against Simon. But before Simon knew what was happening, he slipped his arm under Simon's, pulling the knife away from his throat. In a one-two motion, he drove his elbow hard into Simon's ribs, knocking the breath out of him.

The small figure spun around, dripping blood

from the gash in his arm that Simon's knife must have made. Simon was trying to take a breath when the assailant drove his knee into Simon's crotch. Pain shuddered all the way up Simon's core, and he instinctively knelt down, dropping the knife. The would-be thief punched him once in the face and then sprinted toward the balcony. Simon's pain quickly dissipated, thanks to the IT in his system, and he leapt up and ran after the figure, but by the time he got to the balcony, the intruder was gone.

Simon went over to the railing and looked down. Amid the rain he could see that the figure had already rappelled to the ground, leaving only a black rope and a trail of blood that started where the skirmish began and ended at the edge of the balcony. Simon considered giving chase, but knew he could never get downstairs quickly enough to find the mysterious shadow. He went back into the living room to see if anything was missing.

At the same time, Christine Danam was running up the street, pulling off the black hood and mask she had worn in Simon's apartment.

# EIGHT

Feeling safe in her own place, Chris made sure she had bolted the door and that she was alone. She was still a nervous wreck and shaking from her encounter with Simon.

"Getting fucking sloppy, Chris," she told herself.

She had been bleeding pretty well from the gash on her right forearm. She grabbed her IT pen from the table by the door and held it against the side of her neck. Pressing the button brought the familiar sense of calm and numbness to her body. She started to breathe more slowly and was starting to relax. She'd used her hood as a tourniquet for her right arm, and now she went into the bathroom to wash the wound. She couldn't feel it anymore, but she was worried about how deep the cut was. Pulling her shirt off, she stood in her bra and black pants, facing the mirror that hung over the sink. She held her arm underneath the faucet. Water poured down into the cut, pushing the blood off her arm. The diluted droplets collected in the drain as she used her other hand to push the wound open to see how bad it was. The cut was about two inches long but not as deep as she thought. Simon's knife had only broken the skin, not muscle or bone, but it would need to be stitched.

Opening a drawer in her bathroom, she found a needle and thread. After sterilizing the needle with a lighter, she pushed it through the open wound and back again, weaving a tight crisscross pattern over, under, and through both sides of the open skin. Even with a small-dose IT injection, the pain was considerable, so she gave herself another. Now Chris felt nothing of the needle piercing her skin, dragging with it the thread that cinched the wound together. Her fingers were fumbling, but she was able to make a few fairly neat and clean stitches. She tied off the end of the thread. Reaching to the counter, she grabbed a bottle of disinfectant and spun the cap off with her thumb. She poured it onto the stitched wound and then wrapped her arm with a bandage.

When Chris walked out of the bathroom, she heard her videophone start to ring. She was feeling loopy from the IT but had sense enough to grab a loose-fitting, long-sleeved shirt that was lying nearby and put it on before answering the phone. She didn't even bother to check whom the call was from before she hit the answer button.

"Yeah? Who's there?" she asked.

Rikoh appeared on screen.

"How did it go?"

"Well…it could've gone…better," she said. "There's nothing wrong, but I wasn't able to find the contacts before he woke up. I can try again tomorrow night."

Rikoh thought for a while.

"No," he said. "I have a better idea. Just meet with him tomorrow as planned and get him to come out for the show."

"You seriously want him there?"

"Yes. I think it will work better this way. The doctor is quite interested in Mr. Topaz and wants to meet him in person. I believe if you bring him to the show, it would be the most efficient way."

"So, pardon my language, Rikoh, but how the fuck am I supposed to do that?" Chris asked him, though she knew what he was implying.

Rikoh smirked.

"I'm *sure* you will find a way. Just do it." He ended the call.

"Fucking dickhead," she thought. "This was supposed to be an easy payday, but the rules seem to keep changing." Chris yawned a big yawn. "I swear…if it wasn't…for…the…"

Her exhaustion had caught up with the IT, and she fell into a deep and long sleep.

***

Simon was up and dressed again. After tussling with his faceless intruder, there was no chance of any real sleep that night. He decided to make the most of the time, going back through yesterday's evidence on the Rikoh case. But first, just because he knew it would nag him until he found out, he had to make one call. It was to the building superintendent, an old man named Royal. He found the number in the building's directory menu of his phone and rang him.

"Yeah…um…hello?" answered a frail-sounding voice, an old man's voice.

"Sorry to wake you, Royal. It's Sy. Hey, I know it's early and this all sounds unusual, but do you happen to know if the building's systems were down a few hours ago?"

"Oh…Hey…hey, Sy. Umm, hang on. I can look. Why? Is there a problem?"

Simon decided to keep the break-in to himself. After all, nothing was missing, and he didn't want to cause a panic.

"No. No trouble, Royal. Just seemed to have a glitch earlier. It may have just been me, but I wanted to check."

"Umm…hang on," the old man said.

Simon could hear him fumbling around in the background.

"Nope, no, uh-uh. System reports say everything in the building was secure. You know Mrs. Davis, the widow down on eight? Yeah, she had some trouble the other night too. I brought the programmer back in, and it turned out to be a faulty sensor…You know, with all the rain we've been having, I'm actually surprised the stuff works as well as it does. But nothing but top of the line for my tenants, I always say."

Simon chuckled. "Thanks, Royal. Again, sorry to be bothering you so early like this. I figured it was just something silly, but wanted to make sure."

"Yeah…um…yeah, no problem, Sy. I've been meaning to call you anyway. The missus and I, we do this thing once a year about this time. Nothing much, but we just have some family and friends over. Well, the missus always makes too much food, and all our kids are gone this year. We just wondered if you'd like to join us. It's next weekend…"

"A home-cooked meal does sound really

good, Royal. I'd love to. I'll even bring the wine."

"And maybe a few of those cigars, eh?" Royal asked. "Anyway, yeah…sounds good. Thanks, Sy. Umm…Do you want me to get a programmer down there for ya?"

"Nah. Not right now. I'm sure it'll be fine."

"You sure?" Royal asked. "That little girl that came out to help Mrs. Davis was a right-gone cutie, if ya ask me. Smart, too…Danam, I think her name was."

"Christine Danam?" Simon asked.

"Yeah! You know her?"

"Not personally, but I have heard her name mentioned…Same thing, one of the best security programmers around. Supposedly even worked on stuff for Leader. Ironically, she's stopping by the office tomorrow. I'll just mention it to her then."

"Yeah, yeah. You'll like her, Sy. Great kid, and not too bad on the eyes," said Royal.

"So I hear. Thanks for your help, Royal. Again, sorry to raise you at this hour."

"Hey, no…no problem, Sy. I'll see ya next weekend?"

"I wouldn't miss it. Have a good night—er, morning."

"You too. Call me anytime if it acts up again, and I'll make sure we get it fixed. G'night, Sy."

\*\*\*

Rosalee Sanchez was walking back into the Manna Gallery, terrified of what she might find. The previous night's discovery of a dismembered body was something she had never expected to see, and returning to the scene so soon was making her nervous beyond measure. The police had assured her that this was an idle threat, meant to do nothing more than intimidate her into shutting the exhibit down. The case had probably been brought in by some hooligans from the slums and was nothing more than a sloppy FleshArt display. At least with traditional paintings or photos, art was subjective and depended on what the viewer felt as much as what the artist was trying to convey. With FleshArt, it was different: the best-known artists in that subgenre were skilled surgeons; in fact, that was where the entire culture had come from.

FleshArt was started by medical professionals and popularized by groupies who were into gore and sadism as a means of expressing the wonders of the human body. With the advent of the IT culture, modern medical anesthesia and pain management was so advanced that people willingly gave up their body parts for profit or for new and genetically better parts.

Given the horrors she had become accustomed to viewing in the exhibition, she was surprised that it upset her as much as it did to see a real body. However, the assumptions the police were making and her private talk with Rikoh earlier in the day had convinced her that the show (meaning the exhibit) must go on. She also knew that such things, even if she wasn't used to them, were actually routine...and that extra hit of IT this morning helped calm her nerves quite a bit too.

It was just after four in the morning, and Rosalee had been working at the gallery for an hour or so when she heard the front door open. Peering around the corner, she saw Rikoh with two other men: an impeccably dressed older man who was in great shape and had the face of a god and a middle-aged man with long brown hair pulled back in a ponytail, wearing loose-fitting beige clothing that looked to be made of some twill or natural fiber. She turned the desk lamp in her office off and pulled the door almost completely closed. She was pretty sure that no one saw her, and she would like it to stay that way. After all, being as stoned as she was, she was in no shape to interact with any clientele or patrons. Rikoh and the two men sat in a lounge across the hall from Rosalee's office. She sat in the quiet and eavesdropped on their conversation, being careful not to make any noise that might alert them to her presence.

"So, Andre," said the older man, "from what you and Rikoh have told me, we are all prepared for tonight's floor show."

"Yes, indeed we are, my good doctor," answered Andre. "Our patient is a man named Robert, or 'Bob,' as he calls himself. He is missing his left eye, and the right one is failing him, a result of some sort of accident. Robert agreed to have his right eye removed and donated to our collection, as well as a kidney, which I already have a buyer for. He's already picked out his prosthetic eyes. Anything else you would like to do, Doctor, I leave to your discretion."

"Very good." The doctor smiled.

"I met Mr. Holmsted in my office today, and as part of a 'routine' checkup, I checked his vital functions. His kidneys and liver are in immaculate shape. Seems to be the ideal subject. Rikoh, are we set with getting Topaz to the show?"

"I have someone working on that right now," Rikoh replied.

"Excellent. I want you both to know that it is imperative that Simon Topaz is at tonight's event, but he needs to come of his own free will. I have spent too much time and patience planning everything to have any fuckups now," the doctor said sternly.

He was glaring at Rikoh, and Rikoh knew why.

"I assure you, Dr. Douglas, things will go much smoother than last night. Besides, if that cunt Sanchez hadn't had taken it upon herself to call the cops, I'd say everything else has gone pretty much as you designed it, sir."

Rosalee was horrified when she heard her name mentioned. She wasn't sure what they were talking about or even what Rikoh had or hadn't intended, but she didn't like the feeling that she was part of something sinister.

"Anyway, the cops think it's just a bad FleshArt display sent from a rival gallery," Rikoh said. "I came up with the missing scissors as an excuse to bring Topaz down here, so he would at least be familiar with your work, Dr. Douglas."

Andre laughed.

"What's so funny?" Rikoh asked him.

"A *bad* FleshArt display? That was one of my better pieces. But the police, they're not completely wrong about 'rival' galleries…"

"Andre, thank you for meeting with us. That

will be all for now. I will see you tonight," said Dr. Douglas.

Andre's laugh disappeared as Rikoh smirked. Getting up from his seat, Andre bowed to the doctor. "Until tonight then," he said and walked off, leaving the gallery through the front door.

Thinking they were alone, the doctor turned to face Rikoh.

"Brian," said Rikoh, "I know there have been some missteps, but I assure you everything is still going as planned."

"Very well," Dr. Douglas replied. "Just make sure you deliver Topaz or everything—the money, the girl, what bits of humanity you have left—will be the least of your concerns. Am I clear?"

"Crystal," Rikoh said through clenched teeth.

"Good." Brian smiled and stood. "Now follow me out."

Rosalee could no longer hear them as they began walking toward the front door. She waited until they left, still talking, before she decided to come out of hiding. She didn't like what was going on, not that she understood what was going on. But these people were not good people. She was to meet with this Simon Topaz later in the morning about what she'd seen last night, and she made a mental note of what just took place, just in case. She headed out the front door, touching the pad to lock the door behind her, and briskly walked back to her apartment. She left in such a hurry that she never saw Rikoh walking back toward the gallery.

But Rikoh saw her, and he was getting quite annoyed at the nuisance Ms. Sanchez had become.

# NINE

Simon was sitting in his office, going through the images he had downloaded from his contacts. He was dressed and somewhat refreshed, having taken a shower and dialed in a sizable dose of IT a few hours earlier. Simon never did get any more sleep after his encounter with the mysterious intruder, so he spent the time the best way he knew how: sorting through his notes and discerning what he could from the still images he recorded. Miss Rosalee Sanchez was supposed to meet with him within the hour, so he thought it best to be ready and waiting in his office.

Watching the still images scroll across the screen as he flicked through them with his fingers, he stopped at one in particular that didn't seem right. It was the one of the Blithe family at some family function. He knew who the children were, except for the ten-year-old girl. Looking back through his notes, he realized that there'd been no mention of this child as a victim in the infamous murder.

"Was she just a family friend?" Simon wondered.

He zoomed in on the picture and studied her face. She looked stunningly familiar—like someone he knew but couldn't remember. He took a screenshot of the kid's face and saved it as a different file. Going back through his notes and switching between different pages of information on the screen, Simon tried to find some mention of just who this mystery child might be. In all of the articles and reports written on the Blithe case, there was no information about the family or friends that he didn't already know, and there was certainly nothing about this child. It may be nothing, but Simon had a feeling, and he knew to trust his feelings, however off or strange they might be.

Simon heard the soft ping of the door alarm, and a few moments later, TriXie's voice came through on the intercom.

"MR. TOPAZ, THERE IS A MISS ROSALEE SANCHEZ HERE TO SEE YOU."

"Thank you, TriXie. I'll be right there."

Simon couldn't shake the uneasy feeling he had about the way this case was starting to unfold. Something in his being told him that things were not right, but until he knew more about what was going on, he also knew that he couldn't worry about it. With a few simple keystrokes, the information on the screen went away. It was still ready for him to get back to, but he knew better than to disclose anything that he didn't have to, even if by accident. Getting up from his office chair, he went to a mirror that hung behind the closed office door and made sure he looked presentable. He tucked in his shirt, straightened his tie, and used his fingers to comb his hair.

Opening the door, Simon saw a tall, attractive, olive-skinned woman sitting on a chair in the waiting room. She was wearing a tight white blouse, the buttons of which were straining against two large, obviously fake breasts, and a dark-blue miniskirt that was slit on the side to show off just enough, but not too much, of her well-defined legs. Her body was thin but not skinny, and she had bleached-blond hair and precisely toned makeup that matched her complexion. Simon's first impression was one of a lady who knew her sex appeal and the value it had as a sales tool.

"Miss Sanchez, I presume?"

She grinned, showing off a set of well-kept, perfectly bleached white teeth between her red-painted lips. When she stood, even in heels, she was shorter than Simon, who stood six foot two. He guessed that she was probably five foot eight, plus two inches, if he factored in the stiletto heels she was wearing. She extended a bony hand with long, manicured nails. A diamond tennis bracelet hung off her wrist.

"Yes," she answered. "You must be Simon Topaz. Please, call me Rosalee."

Simon nodded as he shook her hand.

"Thank you, Rosalee, and please…call me Simon. Would you care to step into my office?" he asked, gesturing for her to follow him.

"Certainly."

Rosalee picked up her coat from the arm of the chair, and Simon took it from her and hung it on a peg on the wall, just inside his office door. He shut the door softly behind her.

"Please, have a seat. Can I get you anything to drink?" he asked, nodding toward the display of liquor on the counter.

"No. No, thank you. I'm quite all right."

"Well," Simon said, "I apologize for interrupting your busy schedule. I just have a few questions. As you know, Mr. Rikoh has retained me to find a missing artifact from his exhibit."

Rosalee looked surprised. "I didn't realize there was one missing. He never said anything to me."

"No, he didn't. For security reasons, we felt it best not to discuss this at the gallery, and as of this moment, only three of us—yourself, Rikoh, and I—are even aware that anything is missing."

Her big almond eyes went soft and welled up with tears. Simon could see this, and he handed her a tissue from a box and then went back to his desk chair.

"I certainly hope you don't think I had anything to with it," she said as she wiped her eyes.

"No, not at all," he said. "Quite the contrary, in fact. It's because you weren't aware of it that I wanted to have this interview."

Rosalee nodded.

"So according to Rikoh, the murder weapon on display for the…um…" Simon shuffled through his notes, waiting to see if she would volunteer any information.

Rosalee stayed silent.

"Ah, yes," he said. "The Blithe family murder. Do you happen to know anything about the history of the incident or the weapon?"

"Only what was on display," Rosalee said. "It was a family of five, the parents and three children, including the murderer—the eldest child, Brian Blithe."

"Three children? Total?" Simon asked.

"As far as I know, yes."

"Then you don't know who this is?" Simon pulled a printout of the photo he had been studying just moments before. He pointed at the unknown child.

"No," Rosalee said, looking puzzled. "I've never seen this picture before. Where did you find it?"

"Actually, Rosalee, it was in your vault along with other artifacts deemed too mundane or redundant for your exhibit. You've never seen this before?"

"No, I haven't," Rosalee said. "Rikoh and I went through many documents and artifacts, but I honestly don't recall ever seeing this one." She shook her head. "He's been acting on his own a bit recently, Rikoh has. Maybe he put it in there when I wasn't aware?"

Simon could tell by the stress meter in his contact lenses that Rosalee believed she was telling the truth. She handed the picture back to him, and he put it in the notebook along with his other notes.

"Quite honestly, Mr. Topa—er, Simon," Rosalee said. "I have to admit that with the FleshArt display I found yesterday and something else that happened last night, I'm beginning to regret getting involved with Rikoh's 'business.'"

"What happened last night?"

"It may be nothing, but Rikoh was in the gallery after hours with two other gentlemen."

Rosalee proceeded to tell Simon about the conversation she had overheard a few hours earlier. She told him that his name was mentioned. She also made it clear that she had been hidden the entire time. Simon was furiously writing notes about the encounter, along with the names she mentioned: Andre and a doctor. Simon was starting to believe something that he had already suspected: he had a bigger role in this mystery than just finding a missing artifact. He also realized that Rosalee already knew much more about whatever was going on than Rikoh or his two associates intended her to know. Simon worried, based on what had happened last night, that Rosalee might be in danger, and he told her so.

"Damn peculiar, if you ask me," Simon said. "You're *sure* no one knew you were there or would have been there?"

"Pretty sure," she said. "I left after they had gone, and when I went back later this morning, everything was exactly how I had left it. I haven't seen or heard from Rikoh all day, but that's not unusual. Sometimes, he'll go a couple days without calling or checking in. His checks are good, so I've never really worried about it. To be honest, I always thought the guy was a bit creepy."

Simon cracked a grin. "There's the understatement of the year," he thought.

"Well, like you said, Rosalee, it may be nothing," Simon said. "But I would still feel better if you had some protection. Something really strange is obviously going on, and I fear we just may be a part of it, whether we want to be or not. There's a man with the police, a Detective Mark Riley. I believe you met him yesterday?"

Rosalee nodded as he wrote down Riley's name and number on a small scrap of paper. Simon stood up from his chair and handed her the number.

"I'll contact him after you leave just to keep him apprised of the situation, but I think you would do well to limit your activities until Riley says otherwise."

Rosalee stood as Simon handed her coat to her and opened the door.

"I just had one more question before you go. Do you happen to know the name Christine Danam?" Simon asked.

"No, I don't. Wait...Yes, yes now I remember. She's with Security Concepts. Rikoh had her come in to upgrade MELaNIE. I didn't see much of her, but she seemed to know the system really well. Actually, I'm kind of surprised the security cameras captured nothing; before this exhibit, Rikoh spent a lot of his own money to make sure the building was safe and secure. Why? Do you think she's involved somehow?" Rosalee asked.

They were both standing in the reception area. Simon helped her put on her coat.

"Honestly, I'm not sure," said Simon. "But her name does seem to come up quite a bit. Anyway, as I said, I'll have Detective Riley give you a call. Better to be safe than sorry. Have a great day, Rosalee, and thank you so much for your time."

"No problem. Anything I can do to help, please just ask."

"Will do. Take care, Miss Sanchez."

Simon held the door open for her.

"You too, Simon." She kissed him on the cheek.

He blushed as she smiled and walked away.

Back in his office, Simon punched Riley's number and heard his gruff voice answer.

"Hey, Sy. To what do I owe the honor?"

Simon told Riley about Rosalee's overnight encounter with Rikoh, Andre, and the doctor.

"Yeah," Riley said. "Pretty fucking weird, if youse ask me! I'll get a detail over to hang outside her place…keeps an eye on her. Oh, and Sy, youse know the body? Well, forensics just came back. *None* of the DNA matchy-matchied from…um…part to part, sos to say. Definitely the work of an underground FleshArtist. I'm thinking this Rikoh joker mights be hustlin' two different galleries. But whadda I know, eh?"

"Thanks, Mark," said Simon. "All I know is that something else is going on, and our friend Rikoh seems to be at the center of it."

His interview with Rosalee had left him a lot to think about, and even though it was only noon and he wasn't much of a drinker, he found himself pouring a glass of Scotch. It seemed Rikoh had included him in this game for a purpose, but to what end, he wasn't sure. The screen came back up with all of the documents he had been working on. He knew the picture of the Blithe family was close to four hundred years old, but he still had to check the face of this kid against the New Eden archives. He started the search, and even with today's highly advanced and fast computers, it would take some time for it to match every detail closely enough to give him any viable candidates. The timer on the program counted down from five hours. At four o'clock, he had interview with the security programmer, Christine Danam. In the meantime, he decided to sort through his photos of the case of body parts. FleshArt, Riley had called it.

Doing some research into FleshArt, he came across the basics of the culture, its historical players, and recent news. As best he could tell, FleshArt was still considered an unorthodox and counterculture art form. It had originated with the collection of human art pieces—the tattoos, brandings, and piercings that were collected after a loved one's death to save as mementos. That market, combined with the profitability of organ trafficking and genetically enhanced prostheses lured many a surgeon to FleshArt as an underground means of income.

When the government of New Eden approved the open use of genetically enhanced organs and limbs and decriminalized the cloning of body parts, the time seemed right for what had been an urban myth and underground folktale to become prevalent. The practice wasn't widely known in New Eden because most of its denizens were results of the Genesis program. Ironically, however, it was one of the few things the elite and the lower class shared in common: the elite loved the vivid and scandalous nature of collecting pieces of human beings, and the lower-class citizens did it for the money and to upgrade body parts that were diseased and decaying from living in the slums.

Surgeons were still considered the best FleshArtists, but, as with any art form, many amateurs tried to make their way—usually to the pain and torment of their patient/victims. A surgeon spent years refining his or her touch to make just the right cuts with minimal damage, whereas amateur artists could end up losing a victim to infection or surgical mistakes that did more harm than good. Even within the realm of FleshArt, this was looked down upon. Not so much because of the suffering that the victim endured but because good natural body parts were hard to come by, and to waste a finite resource was just…inefficient.

Genetically enhanced organs, which were made through an artificial cloning process, worked better than their natural counterparts did, but, especially in the slums, it was cost prohibitive. The elite and super-rich ruling classes could afford replacement parts, and they made sure that the power stayed among the few families that occupied their ranks. With new parts, it was easy for someone's lifespan to double or triple, making some in the upper echelon almost two hundred years old—with the fitness and virility of someone in his teens. Simon was intrigued. How many people did he know who might actually be cloners? He wasn't sure of anyone in particular, nor did he really suspect anyone, but it did speak a lot to the nature of politics, money, and medicine in New Eden. He didn't doubt that many government representatives, as far up as Leader, were able to stay in their positions so long simply because they got replacement organs at the first sign of trouble. The only organ that couldn't be replaced or modified was the brain.

It was quickly approaching 4:00 p.m., and Simon had been lost in thought and research. This whole new world of FleshArt and the submarkets it spawned was fascinating. When he noticed the clock, he decided to check on his facial-recognition program. It still had at least two hours to process. The door alarm and TriXie had both told Simon, within a few seconds of each other, that the enigma known as Christine Danam was now standing in his reception area. Again, he checked his appearance quickly and opened the door.

Before him, with her back to the door, stood a small woman with purple hair, wearing jeans and a long-sleeved T-shirt. When she turned, Simon was caught off guard by her beauty. This was the woman of his dreams…quite literally. It was *her* face that had replaced Anne's during his IT-inspired hallucination last night. He was lost for words.

"Simon Topaz?" Chris asked as she smiled and put her hand out to shake his.

He couldn't quit staring at her, and it took him a moment to compose himself. Chris stood there worried that he somehow recognized her from last night. She began to withdraw her hand slowly as Simon realized he hadn't said anything yet.

"Yes! Yes…Hi. You must be Christine." He was lost in her eyes, never losing contact with them, but he had the presence of mind to put his hand out to shake hers.

Chris realized that Simon didn't recognize her and that instead, he seemed enamored of her. She was used to men making a fuss over her, but he was different. There was a certain gentleness and sadness in his eyes. She could see it beyond the contacts, which he failed to hide and which she had failed to steal. But now she was here with a different purpose. She blushed and pushed her hair behind her ear.

Simon realized he was gawking for too long and she had noticed. "Focus!" his inner voice screamed.

He smiled. She smiled back at him.

"Wow," she thought. "This will be easier than I expected. But at the same time, he's really cute. I don't know what Rikoh wants with him, but this might be more fun than I thought."

"Thank you for coming. Won't you come in, Miss…uh…Dana—"

"Chris," she interrupted him. "You can just call me Chris. Everyone does."

"Okay," Simon said. "Chris, please just call me Simon."

"Oh, I think we can do better than that…"

"Is she flirting with me?" wondered Simon.

"Sy. All my friends call me Sy."

"Am I flirting with him?" wondered Chris.

"So I get to be your friend, then? That's good!" she said.

"Well, if you were my enemy, you'd be the best-looking one yet."

"Great…*very* subtle, Sy!" he admonished himself.

She rolled her eyes but then stared right back at him and bit her lip as she laughed. "So why am I here, Sy?"

Simon knew he needed to get down to business, so he did. He led her into the office, poured a drink, scotch on the rocks, for each of them, and handed her a glass before sitting in the chair adjacent to hers. She sipped her drink.

Leaning forward, he was upfront with her. "I was retained by Rikoh, who I know you're familiar with. He hired you to upgrade the security at the Manna Gallery a few months back. He's asked me to find an artifact that's gone missing." Simon had been staring into space until then; he looked her in the eyes again. "A murder weapon."

The smile left her face.

"Murder weapon?" she asked.

"Yeah, the exhibit he's funding…it's a collection of antique memorabilia from infamous murders about four hundred years ago."

She shook her head. "I always figured that guy was a little twisted…What does this have to do with me?"

"Well," Simon said, sipping his drink. "You are one of three people who had access to the item."

"I've never taken anything from the gallery."

He knew that was a true statement; his contacts confirmed it.

"I didn't think that you had," said Simon, "but you're the only one who would know how to bypass the security system, and someone has doctored the footage."

Her eyes grew wide. She didn't know what was going on, but if she wanted to keep getting IT, Andre had told her, she needed to keep Rikoh happy…short of sleeping with him. Andre could be a bastard, but he was still her brother. She decided to come clean. "Rikoh asked me to erase the footage."

Simon was floored. He didn't expect this, and he certainly didn't expect her to tell him upfront the way she had.

"Do you know why? Did he steal anything from the gallery?"

"I don't really know why, but he told me…he told me that my brother could get in a lot of trouble."

"What does your brother have to do with this?" Simon asked.

"My brother, Andre, is one of the premier exhibitors of FleshArt. He's been doing business with Rikoh for years. When Rikoh went to Manna with this exhibit, we were actually kind of surprised. We thought we had a good rapport with Rikoh. Listen…" Chris leaned forward and touched Simon's hand. "My brother has been trying to buy Manna for years, but that bitch, Sanchez, is too stubborn to sell. Rikoh wasn't happy with the business he was doing with Sanchez, so they decided to scare her by putting an FA fixture up in the middle of the night. It was supposed to look like a…actually, I don't know how it was supposed to work. A prank, I guess. It was all Rikoh's idea, anyway."

Simon stood and walked around to the seat behind his desk. He sat down and started making notes.

"Please, Sy. Don't say anything. If you go to the police, I'll deny it all."

She was serious. He quit writing and nodded.

"Does the video show either of them taking

anything from the gallery?"

She looked puzzled and ashamed. "Taking? No. No, all they did was put the case in the room, and Rikoh asked me to delete the footage of them doing it."

"Why?" asked Simon.

"I told you, so they wouldn't get in trouble."

Something in the stress meter was reading higher than usual. She wasn't lying, but Simon knew she wasn't telling him everything. He thought for a minute.

"You said that your brother, Andre, is well versed in FleshArt. Do you think I could talk to him? I won't mention what you told me. I only have some questions about FleshArt that I need answered."

"Yeah, I don't see why not, if it's *just* about FleshArt."

Simon nodded.

"Actually," said Chris, "he's holding a live demonstration in about two hours at his gallery. I've seen it a million times, but would you like to see it and meet him afterward?"

"Now?" Simon hesitated for only a second. "Yeah. Let me grab my coat."

The mood seemed light again. They were both thinking the same thing but for entirely different reasons. One word crossed both of their brains at the same time: perfect.

Simon led Chris out of the office. He never saw that his computer had finished its query and that the information on the screen named *him* as the closest match to the girl in the photo.

# TEN

Simon and Chris stepped out of the cab and walked through the row of abandoned shops and warehouses. Only one building at the end of the street was lit up, and it seemed that all the activity for miles around was focused on this one spot. As they got closer, Chris stopped Simon and pulled him around the corner of another building. She opened her small backpack and pulled out two face masks, one purple and one green. The masks were of a masquerade style, covering only the eyes and nose. A soft plastic band wrapped around the back of the head to keep the mask secure.

"Here," Chris said, handing the green mask to Simon. She pulled the straps on hers to make sure it was snug. "We'll need these. It's customary for guests to wear masks, and even if you recognize someone, don't call them out by name. FleshFaires have always been steeped in anonymity. It's the one thing that makes people feel safe to come out and watch."

Simon fumbled with his mask, and Chris put her hands behind his head to help him cinch the strap. Simon gazed into her eyes again. She was beautiful, no doubt. But he also felt a sense of calm comfort from her. It was a feeling he had not had since his beloved Anne had left.

Catching his gaze, she felt something, a feeling she had never really known before, stir inside her. It was a warmth and elation that somehow Simon was directing her to feel, just through the will of his eyes. He put his hands up to touch hers and held them as she pulled them away slowly.

The tender moment was suddenly broken when, as she was pulling her hands away, her shirtsleeve fell down far enough to expose the bandage on her forearm. She yanked her hands away and put on her backpack, moving with fluidity so as not to draw attention to the injury. Chris hoped he hadn't seen it, but Simon had, and all at once, he realized that he had met Chris before. His mind flashed back to the events of the early morning—the struggle with and the disappearance of his mysterious intruder.

In a split second, so many of his questions were answered, but just as many new ones were raised. She was quick and clever, but Simon was on full alert. Now he doubted the reasons and motives behind Miss Danam's charm. He decided to play ignorant until he could get more information from her. If nothing else, she surely owed him an explanation. The pair continued to walk toward the building, Andre's gallery.

Chris decided to break the tension. "Just so you know, there aren't many rules for this type of performance."

"What does that mean?" asked Simon.

"It means that you should realize that you're

about to watch a live, technically illegal surgery. This isn't for the queasy or faint of heart. Although our artists are some of the best in the world, it will still be gory, and not everyone can handle it. If you feel like you need to be sick, we ask that you try to excuse yourself."

Simon nodded. He was still trying to process the fact that this sweet, beautiful girl was the same person who was searching his apartment and beat the shit out of him a few hours earlier. He couldn't help bringing it up.

"Hey, if you don't mind me asking, I noticed you had a large bandage on your arm. What happened?"

Chris stiffened as she frantically tried to make up an excuse. She managed a fake, forced laugh, pulled her sleeve up, and pointed it out.

"This?" she said. "Oh, this is just one of the joys of being a cat lover."

It was a complete and utter lie, both she and Simon knew, but he was content in leaving the matter alone…for the moment.

*** 

The decline of the truck dock had been filled in with stairs and ramps, allowing people to walk directly onto the showroom floor. The stage was lit with dim blue lights that revealed objects of different sizes hidden under black cloth. A large table sat in the middle of the stage. Soft music of guitars, flutes, and drums played over the speakers suspended high above the stage. On each side of the stage was a large screen. There was no image on either one.

People were filling the theater-style seating.

All, like Simon and Chris, were wearing masks of different colors and styles. Simon followed Chris to the side of the stage, where a tall set of rolling stairs had been placed. Walking behind her, he had a great view of the stage and the audience. At the top of the mezzanine, which was blocked by a guardrail, there was a single row of chairs. These were much more ornate and appeared to be more comfortable than the others were. To the left of the seats and projecting over the center of the stage was a small thrust, just big enough for one person to stand on. A microphone on a stand had been placed on it.

Simon sat in the seat nearest the staircase, and Chris took the seat next to him. "Great seats," he joked.

Chris chuckled. "Yeah, well, it helps to know people."

As the last few people took their seats, the large roll-up doors began to close. It was a capacity crowd, but it totaled no more than a hundred. Chris relaxed in her seat, so Simon did likewise. The music began to swell, and a chorus of people chanting in a foreign language joined the instruments.

Attendants dressed in black and wearing black masks walked out onto the stage and removed the black cloths, exposing the objects beneath them: a tray of surgical instruments; a hook for IV bags; a small monitor displaying respiration and heart rates, as well as blood pressure and other vital functions; and finally, a set of large gas canisters with plastic tubing that ran to different machines. It was, for all intent and purpose, a modern reproduction of a twenty-first-century operating room.

Suddenly, the music gained momentum, and the stage lights started to twirl and change color. Footlights snapped on, and four young, attractive women entered, two from each side of the stage. They were wearing only see-through plastic scrubs, and they danced in a choreographed set of ballet moves and acrobatic tumbling in sync with the music. On the mezzanine, to Simon's left, a lone door opened. Out walked a thin man with long brown hair. He wore a purple suit, covered by a long, flowing purple robe. He was carrying a cane topped with a large crystal jewel, and he was the only person in the room who was not wearing a mask. Chris started to clap, as did the rest of the audience, as Andre strolled out onto the thrust and stood in front of the microphone. The show was about to begin.

The lights above the stage settled to bathe it in bright, white light. A set of spotlights converged on Andre and made him shine alone in the darkness that enveloped the mezzanine. He indulged in the applause for a few moments before raising his hand. As his hand went up, the room fell quiet, and the music faded into the background. The room was cold—cold enough that Simon could see Andre's breath as he spoke into the microphone.

"Ladies and gentlemen, boys and girls, and monsters of all ages, welcome to the menagerie!"

The crowd cheered and applauded. Andre began to talk over the buzz, and the mood quickly calmed in the room.

"Tonight, my faithful few, we have quite the show for you. Nurses, if you would?"

Everyone watched as the four young women took positions around the operating table. A set of double doors on the left corner of the stage opened, and two more nurses, wearing sheer, white scrubs and white face masks, pushed a gurney onto the stage. Strapped to the gurney was a small man, wearing only a thin hospital gown and a patch over one eye. He was gagged and thrashing about, clearly in a panic. Seeing the silhouettes of shadow people only made his agitation worse. Tears flowed from his working eye, and his muffled screams for help turned into dire sobs. Simon was getting anxious about what was about to happen.

Chris could see him from the corner of her eye and whispered, "Relax. It's all part of the show."

Simon took little comfort in knowing that, but he did his best to sit and watch. Andre, lit by a spotlight and standing twenty feet tall on the large screens, said, "Our very special patient tonight lost an eye in an industrial accident. Such a pity...When he heard of our special work, he was only too anxious to trade in his other eye for two new, state-of-the-art Maxwell Oculus-3000s! My friends, please welcome our very, very special guest and a dear, personal friend: Robert!"

A man dressed in red surgical scrubs and red face mask walked onto the stage and injected Bob Holmsted in the neck with a needle. Unceremoniously, Bob's pupil widened, and then he was in the deep trance of a surgical-strength IT hold. Bob was still conscious, but he was relaxed and sedated. He no longer struggled against his bonds.

The nurses unlatched his restraints, and the six of them slid Bob from the gurney onto the operating table in the center of the stage. The images on the screens switched between camera views of Bob, the nurses prepping for the surgery, and the man in the red scrubs checking the valves and dials on the gas canisters. Both screens then switched back to Andre, and the focus of the audience was again on him.

"So, without further ado, please welcome our guest artist from our very own CS214, the maestro of surgical talent...*Dr. D!*"

With a flourish of lights and pounding electronic music, Brian Douglas walked onto the stage wearing red scrubs and a mask that made his face resemble a skull with living eyes. The spotlights pulled away from Andre and focused on Brian, who bowed to the audience before walking over to the operating table, where the rest of the cast had positioned themselves around Bob's drugged-up body. The screens showed Bob's vital signs superimposed on the image of Bob lying on the table. The other man in red turned the valves of the gas canisters, removed Bob's gag, and replaced it with a gas mask. Bob's eye slowly fluttered, and he was asleep. The nurses had been setting probes and sensors all over Bob's body, and those were now starting to feed data to the monitoring equipment. A nurse plugged IV lines into Bob's veins, and then they were ready. Simon looked over to where Andre had been standing and noticed that he was gone. Looking down onto the stage, Simon could see Andre's shadowed form—he had already made it downstairs and was watching the event from just offstage, cloaked in darkness. Dr. D made his way over to Bob and looked down at him. He held out his hand, asked the nurse for a scalpel, and began to work.

\*\*\*

Five hours into the surgery, Dr. D had made steady progress. He had removed Bob's working eye and prepared to retrofit a new, cloned "supereye" in its place. He was finishing the procedure when he suddenly stopped. He looked up into the set of seats in the mezzanine. Simon knew that Dr. D couldn't see past the lights, but from the direction he was staring, Simon had the uneasy feeling that the doctor was looking at him. Chris also sensed that something was amiss. She needed to talk to Andre.

"Wait here a minute. I'll be right back," she said as she got up.

"What's wrong?" Simon asked.

"Probably nothing, but I need to speak to Andre really quick."

Before Simon could protest, Chris had already made her way across the mezzanine and through the doorway. Simon looked down at the stage again. The audience was murmuring. Dr. D looked at his assistant.

"Wake him up," he said.

The assistant and nurses looked at Dr. D in horror.

"We're not finished yet," the assistant surgeon said. "If you pull him out now, he'll feel everything."

"I said *wake him up!*" Dr. D shouted.

Members of the audience were now starting to

get to their feet. Simon could see Andre and Chris arguing off the side of the stage. Andre walked out on stage causally and smiled at the audience.

"Ladies and gentlemen, please…please take your seats."

"What the *fuck* are you doing?" Andre whispered to Dr. D, as he smiled and waved at the audience.

People were starting to leave, and no one on stage had honored Dr. D's request yet. They all stood there frozen, staring at him. Dr. D went over to the tray and picked up a syringe of bright-yellow liquid. The assistant surgeon tried to stop him, but Dr. D suddenly head butted him, knocking him backward.

Simon was now on his feet. As he made his way toward the stairwell, a nurse screamed, and people started running. Suddenly, the roll-up doors opened, and a bevy of police officers stormed in.

People were fleeing in an absolute panic. Dr. D injected Bob with the yellow serum as Simon made his way down to the stage. People were running around like mad. They were being chased and subdued by the police. Just as Simon reached the stage, Bob sat up, screaming in ungodly agony, clutching and clawing at his missing eyes. Simon met the gaze of Dr. D for a split second before he saw the doctor make a daring leap off the edge of the stage and run back through the doors of the office.

Simon felt a sharp electrical pulse course through his neck, and his knees gave way as he blacked out. Rikoh was standing over Simon's unconscious body when Andre ran over and tackled him.

"You dirty son of a bitch!" Andre yelled as he punched Rikoh in the face. "You fucking ruined me!"

Chris had made it over too late to warn Simon. Andre was taking out his frustration on Rikoh, and cops were arresting people. She decided to grab Simon's unconscious body.

Rikoh managed to get to his feet, and he ran toward the door through which Dr. D had exited. Andre was on his heels, and they disappeared into the gallery. How Chris was able to hold Simon's semiconscious body up and drag him outside without getting caught, she'll never know, but she had managed it. She was able to prop him up well enough in front of her on her motorcycle, and she rode away. No one followed.

Meanwhile, the nurses cried as Bob slumped over dead. His heart had given out from the pain.

# ELEVEN

Andre was frightened, furious, and thought that somehow, Rikoh and Brian Douglas had slipped out of the building unnoticed. After checking for them outside and catching sight of the police loading their paddy wagons with members of his audience, Andre knew there was only one secure place for him to hide out, even though it was right in the middle of the storm.

"The eye is always the calmest place," he thought.

He crawled back into the building through a secret panel that opened onto the stairwell leading up to his office. Andre always had safeguards in place, just in case there was a raid. At most, the police would find the gallery and the showroom, but his office was his sanctuary, and he made sure to keep it well hidden. He quickly pushed on a cement door that was hinged just so and hidden among the boxes and debris at the bottom of the stairwell. When it was sealed, no one could tell from the other side that it wasn't just a continuous run of the wall and that a staircase lay behind it. Sweaty and in a panic, Andre heaved his body against the cement slab, hoping it would take days for the authorities to find him there—especially if they weren't looking.

Exhausted and out of breath, he made his way up the stairs and into the small common area just outside his office. The upper stairwell door closed behind him, but he was surprised and a bit nervous when he heard it lock. Someone was up there with him. But who?

"Did Chris make it out okay?" he wondered.

Andre walked toward his office slowly and saw Brian sitting in a chair, facing him, across the room. Brian simply smiled, which brought back the anger that Andre had forgotten in his panic.

"You have a lot of explaining to do," Andre said, quickening his pace. "What the fuck was all that about—"

Before he could get the question out and just as he stepped over the threshold, a quick sting pierced the back of his neck. He felt the IT start to take over his system in much too strong a wave. He spun around just in time to see Rikoh standing behind him with an injection pen. Then the muscles in his legs gave out, and he collapsed in a heap on the floor.

\*\*\*

Simon opened his eyes slowly and found himself lying on a couch in a small but well-furnished apartment. There was a cat standing on his chest, licking his cheek. His head pounding with a slow, heavy thud that matched his heartbeat. When he tried to lift himself, intense pain screamed across his arms and neck.

"Nino, no! Shoo!"

Chris ran over to the couch and picked the cat up. She could tell that Simon was in a great deal of pain. Simon was surprised but not shocked when she pulled his injection pen from her pocket. She knelt at his side and held the pen where he could see it.

"How much?" she asked.

He was barely able to speak. The pain in his body held him down as though he were a prisoner in his own body. "Four," he muttered with what little energy he had left.

"You only have two mics left."

Tears welled up in Simon's eyes. A two-microgram dose would be enough to hold the DTs at bay, but not nearly enough to give him the strength to get on his feet. Chris set the dial to four anyway. She held the pen up to his neck but saw him whisper "no" before pushing the button. She understood: the heaviest IT users couldn't get a reaction fast enough by injecting the drug into a limb or even the neck.

"Where?" she asked.

"He...hear...heart."

The word barely rolled out of Simon's mouth. His body was so racked with pain that he couldn't yell or scream. At best, he could moan as tears flowed freely from his eyes. Chris looked at him with a genuine concern and quiet desperation. She unbuttoned his shirt to reveal his bare, scar-covered chest. There was a small *X* tattooed directly above his heart. From the round scars and scabs that were there, she knew this was the place.

She pushed the pen firmly to his chest and pressed the button. Within seconds, he was able to move, albeit slowly and clumsily. He was able to sit up, but the signs of pain on his face softened her resolve to hold any secrets from him. She got up, walked over to a table near the front door, and pulled out her own injection pen. She knelt down at his feet again. She showed him her pen.

"It's street. Is that okay?" she asked.

Simon nodded, and Chris set the dial on her own pen to three before pushing it up against his chest and pushing the button. In two heartbeats, color and composure returned to Simon's face. She set the pen on the coffee table. Simon's breathing went from quick and shallow to slow, even, and deliberate breaths. She held his hand as they both stood up.

"I was worried I might have—"

Before Chris could say more, Simon lurched forward and embraced her in a tight hug.

"Lost you," Chris said. His gesture caught her by surprise, but she brought her arms up slowly and wrapped them around him, laying her head on his chest. His arms were strong and inviting. She felt safe being held by them.

"When I brought you here," she said, the two of them still holding one another, "I sat you on the couch, and the pen fell out of your pocket. I…I knew what it was, and I knew you'd be in pretty rough shape, depending on when you last dosed."

Simon broke his hold around her, and she did likewise. They stared into each other's eyes. Suddenly, Simon moved his hands to cup her face and kissed her.

Chris was even more surprised by the kiss than she was by the hug. Simon's tongue began exploring her mouth, and she let it, quickly following with hers. Chris put her arms around Simon's neck and drew him closer. She wasn't sure what this meant, if anything; she just knew it felt right. The kiss only lasted a few seconds, and then Simon let his forehead rest against Chris's. Their noses touched. He looked her in the eyes as he whispered, "Thank you."

Chris stuck her tongue out just enough to moisten her lips.

"Yeah...No problem," she said. They smiled in unison.

She reached down, grabbed her injection pen from the table, and slid it into her pocket. Simon began to button his shirt while Chris turned and walked into the kitchen.

"Where are we?" he asked.

"My place," she said. "Would you like something to drink?"

"Yes, please," he replied.

Simon wasn't sure what had come over him—if it was just the stress of the last few days or the fact that it had been years since he was last with a woman—but everything had felt so right and proper since he met Chris. Simon knew, however, that there were still some unanswered questions.

"You know, not to put a damper on the mood, but I still have some questions for you Chris."

Chris set two wine glasses on the table and filled them half full.

"Oh?" She said.

Simon had moved to the couch. Chris sat beside and facing him, her leg tucked underneath her and a glass of wine in her hand.

"Shoot," she said.

Simon turned to look at her when he asked

her, "Why did you break into my apartment?"

Chris answered with a question of her own. "What makes you think I did?"

"Well, for starters, the wound on your arm. If it was bad enough to require a bandage, I don't suspect it was from the cat. Then there's the fact that you work for Security Concepts and were the one who programmed the security systems in my building."

"I program for a lot of buildings," she said. "But go on."

Simon smiled. "Then there was right now. When I held you, I knew it was you."

Chris brushed her hair back behind her ear and smiled.

"Rikoh asked me to," she confessed. "He knew you were wearing tech-enhanced contacts when you met with him. He wanted me to download the data and find out what you knew."

"So, what did I know?" Simon asked.

"Beats me. You caught me before I had the chance to do anything. Can I ask you something?"

"Sure," said Simon.

"Would you have really stabbed me?"

Simon thought for a second. "No," he said flatly. "I wasn't expecting any visitors at that hour so…well, you know."

They smiled at each other.

"Not that I even could have," he added. "I seem to remember you had quite the punch." He took a sip of his wine.

"Well, you know…" Chris said, mocking him.

"A girl's gotta protect herself." She set her drink down and inched closer to him. "Was there anything else you realized when you held me?"

Simon set his drink down also. "Only this," he said as they both leaned into another passionate kiss.

She pushed so hard against him that she fell on top of him. They both smiled between feverous kisses. The cat jumped onto the couch and tried to wedge her way between them. They both laughed as Chris stood up, took Simon's hand, and led him to her bedroom. The cat followed, but Chris pushed the door closed before she could enter. Nino waited at the door for a few seconds before recognizing that he'd been shut out. She turned around, leapt onto the couch, and nestled himself in the warm spot where Simon had been sitting.

\*\*\*

Rosalee Sanchez was in her apartment, trying to calm her nerves. She wasn't sure whom she could trust and whom she couldn't, but one thing was painfully clear: she had been manipulated this entire time to carry out other people's plans, and she had no idea why. She really didn't care why; she just hated the feeling, and it was making her overly suspicious of everyone and everything. Peeking out the window between the curtains, she saw the two men whom Detective Mark Riley had sent over earlier in the day. They were sitting in a causal black sedan. If she didn't know these men were here specifically to guard her, she never would have noticed their presence, let alone their purpose.

Rosalee took another drag from the vapor-pod she held in her hand and let the breath out slowly. The flavor was sweet, but the chemicals were a combination of popular sedatives and central nervous system depressants so she could put herself at ease. IT was relaxing, but it also made her feel hyperfocused, and any break she could get from this week's stress would be a welcome feeling. Her videophone began to ring. It was Rikoh. Rosalee debated whether to answer the call, but she also knew she didn't want to make him suspicious of her. She touched the answer button.

Rikoh appeared on screen as disheveled as she had ever seen him. He still had his neat appearance, but there was a small bandage over his left eye, and his hair had fallen down around the sides of his face, something she had never seen in the few weeks she had known him.

"Rosalee."

"He never calls me by my first name," she thought.

"Rosalee, I'm glad I found you at home at this hour. Forgive the intrusion, but a critical business matter regarding the financial future of Manna Gallery has arisen. I wondered if you would be available to meet with my primary investor."

Rosalee, aided by the pod she was smoking, decided to act cool and ignorant.

"Sure," she said. "When?"

"Unfortunately, time is of the essence, so I was wondering if you could meet us at his house now. I took the liberty of sending a car for you. It should be there within moments."

"Rikoh, it's late. Are you sure it can't wait

until morning?"

"Quite sure. He is departing for Oceania in the morning and needs clarification on some financial matters concerning the gallery. I do not have the latest data; only you do, and instead of wasting the time it would take for me to compile it for him, I felt it best if you could meet us."

"You know the police are here, watching me, right? It might be suspicious if I left right now without letting them know where I'm going."

"I was not aware, but I will let Detective Riley know. Either way, it should not take more than an hour away from your evening."

It was against her better judgment, but lest she make him suspicious…and she wasn't even *sure* that something bad was going on…

"Fine. I'll be there shortly."

"Very good. I thank you, Miss Sanchez."

Between the calming effects of the drug that she was inhaling and her own self-doubts, she felt better about going to see Rikoh. She did have enough presence of mind to contact one person first, just in case something was off. She dialed the number, and it rang through five times before a message answered: "Hi, this is Simon. Sorry I missed your call, but leave a message, and I'll return it as soon as I can."

*** 

On a nightstand next to Christine Danam's bed, the screen on Simon's phone lit up, but no sound was made. He had turned the ringer off earlier when watching the floorshow and never had a chance to turn it back on. His interest was nowhere near work anyway. In that moment, there were only two people in the world: Chris and him.

They had both taken their shoes off when they first entered her bedroom, which wasn't easy, considering they didn't want to take their hands off one another or stop the frantic and passionate kissing. Chris was lying on the bed with Simon partly off to her side and partly on top of her. His hands were caressing her back, occasionally moving down to her hips and back up again. She had unbuttoned his shirt and helped pull it off his shoulders. She could feel the raised scar tissue that was embossed across his entire torso: his shoulders and upper arms, his chest, and his back, stopping just short of his neck. She used her fingertips to draw invisible lines around his upper body.

As they continued to kiss, he put his hands underneath her shirt to feel the bare, soft skin of her back. It was then that he realized she wasn't wearing a bra and brought his hands around to her chest. His large hands cupped her small breasts. He used his thumb to trace circles around her hard, pierced nipples while pinching them with his index and middle fingers. When he did this, he could feel her moan in his mouth. Her breathing began to quicken as her chest moved in time.

Simon pulled his hands away from her breasts and moved his fingers slowly across her flat stomach to the waistband of her jeans. He unthreaded her belt and cinched it just a bit tighter to get the pin to disengage. Her belt loosened as she pulled her hands away from his back to help pull the button and unzip her jeans. He reached along the sides of her jeans and put his fingers just inside the waistband. Pushing her jeans and panties down in one motion, Chris lifted her hips to give Simon unobstructed space. She pulled her legs out of her jeans one at a time, and he tossed the garments off the side of the bed.

Simon's kisses broke away from Chris's mouth and drifted down her chin to her neck. He pulled his body down, and hovering over her, used his used his teeth to lightly bite her hard nipples through her shirt. Chris whimpered in pleasure and ran her fingers through his hair. Simon looked back up at her for a moment, and they both giggled before he continued.

Sitting up, Simon held one of Chris's legs and rested the other on his shoulder. He kissed her ankles, leaving her socks on, and slowly started to move up her legs, kissing the insides of her calves, then the insides of her knees, alternating between legs. Sliding his upper body so his shoulders pushed against the back of her thighs, he moved from kissing the insides of her legs to the top of her clean-shaven and tattooed pubic mound. Hearing Chris moan, he started running his tongue across the outer edge of her labia. Simon used his tongue to map her lower lips. She pushed her fingers through his hair and grabbed the back of his head as he, at the same time, pushed his tongue deep inside her. He could taste her essence as her hips bucked—her juices dampening his chin and his nose flicking across her clitoris. As he began using the tip of his tongue to caress her clit, she let out a large gasp and pushed his head closer in.

"Oh my God, that feels so good!"

She moaned as he continued pushing his

tongue down, using the flat side of it to run the entire length of her vagina. Simon pushed her legs back and bent his head down so his tongue could run along the edge of her anus. She squealed as he pleasured her for close to ten minutes. A few minutes into the act, his fingers found their way inside her, pushing in and pulling out, faster and faster, as his tongue alternated between her holes. She was at the brink, wrapping her legs around his head and squeezing tighter and tighter as the words "fuck," and "yes," and "God" escaped between heavy breaths. He could feel her shudder as she screamed and bucked violently.

Simon sat up, his face wet with Chris's climax. As he used the back of his arm to wipe most of it away, she was frantically trying to get his pants off. She could feel his hardness through his slacks as they switched places in bed and he helped her to remove the garments. He was fully nude, except for his socks, and she could now see where the scars ran down and pitted the pubic area around his large penis. He only had one testicle; Sindel's thugs had unceremoniously removed the other many years ago. She stared at his manhood long enough and with such an odd expression that he began to feel ashamed. He moved his legs up toward his chest to cover himself. Chris looked at him, and realizing her mistake and his embarrassment, she quickly grabbed his dick, which was still rock hard, and straddled him, pulling him inside her. He was larger than average, and in a similar example of fate (or perhaps nature's folly) she was tighter than any woman he'd been with before. She thrust so hard onto him initially that he had no time to react.

Chris leaned down with Simon still inside her and kissed him more passionately than she had ever before. Simon no longer felt the shame of the condition of his skin and pulled her close to him, holding her tighter than he had before. She had barely noticed, as they were trying to weld their bodies together with sheer will, that he had pulled all but the head of his dick from inside her. They were both in the throes of ecstasy as they kissed, and he thrust hard, pushing himself into her as deep as he could go. She had no choice but to break away from his mouth to let out a giant moan.

The pair continued to pleasure each other for over an hour, only stopping when Simon finally tensed up. Chris was now on her back and Simon on top of her, when she knew by his body language that he was ready to cum. Wrapping her legs around him tightly and looking into his eyes, she whispered, "Cum inside me."

He did just that, exploding inside her at the same time she felt herself climax for the fifth time that night. With a roar, he fell down onto the bed. Both of them were drenched in sweat. Neither one had let go of the other for more than a few seconds the entire time they made love. Simon was lying with Chris at his side, her head on his chest, when he started chuckling to himself.

Chris, smiling, looked up at him.

"What?" she asked.

Simon just shook his head. "I was just thinking about a dream I had last night. Actually, it was more a vision I had before I caught you in my place."

Chris sat up and looked at him as he said, "I think I've always known you…and somehow I've always known." He paused.

"Known what?" she asked.

"That I've always loved you."

She smiled and kissed him. "I'm going to jump in the shower," she said, pulling off her shirt as she got out of bed.

He stared at her, amazed, and watched her as she walked around to his side of the bed. He laughed again.

"Now what?" she asked, kneeling next to him.

He rolled over and looked her in the eye. "You're so…You are simply magnificent," he stated simply.

She smiled widely. "So are you," she said.

*** 

Simon and Chris were lying in bed, asleep and holding one another, when Simon was startled awake by a bright, flashing light from the nightstand. It was his phone, and it was Riley, calling at an ungodly hour. He made sure the phone was video muted and quietly made his way out of bed and out of the room, being extra careful not to wake Chris.

About ten minutes later, Chris awoke, noticing Simon was no longer next to her. She sat up. The bedroom door was cracked open, and she could see light coming from living room. She got out of bed and walked into the living room to find Simon sitting on the couch with his phone to his ear.

Simon hit the end button when he heard

something stir behind him. He looked over his shoulder to see Chris standing there in her robe.

"Is everything okay?" she asked.

He looked weary and pained. "No."

She walked over and sat on the couch next to him. "What's going on?"

He held her hands in his. "That was my contact with the police. They just found your brother…I'm sorry…"

Chris's eyes welled up with tears as she shook her head and kept saying, "No."

Simon pulled her close to him as she started sobbing. His phone was sitting on the table, but he still hadn't noticed the message that Rosalee had left for him a few hours before.

# TWELVE

Rosalee got out of the car and walked up a small path to the only gate in the long fence that surrounded the large, ornate house. Looking over her shoulder, she could see the officers that Riley had provided for her protection park their black sedan across the street. Only moments ago, she had told the men inside the car that she was just going to a business meeting, but they insisted on following her. Just knowing they were close made her more comfortable with this meeting.

She pressed a button on the panel and heard a voice from the other side of the gate. "Miss Sanchez! Thank you coming on such short notice!"

Rikoh was standing inside the gate and swung it open to greet her. A sudden flash of lightning and a roll of thunder frightened Rosalee—it made her jump. She noticed the wind picking up speed and throwing leaves around the yard.

"Rikoh!" she exclaimed. "You scared me!"

Rikoh was holding the gate open as Rosalee walked past him.

"My apologies. I saw you on the monitor coming up toward the house and decided to meet you out here. Quickly, let's get inside before the storm hits."

Rikoh's demeanor made Rosalee suspicious. He was acting quite friendly and casual, something not so strange in and of itself, but in her experience with Rikoh, it was peculiar. As if on cue, the skies opened and heavy sheets of rain poured down. Rosalee had no choice but to jog with Rikoh to the shelter of the porch. He approached and opened the door into the house, motioning for Rosalee to enter first. She did, but she made sure to keep some distance between Rikoh and herself. The house was warm and inviting. Rikoh and Rosalee were standing in what appeared to be the kitchen.

"Here, let me take your coat," he offered.

Rosalee, nervous and skeptical, allowed him to. She had pulled her arm out of one sleeve of her jacket when she felt Rikoh lurch and the quick sting of something biting her neck. She could barely turn around before everything went dark, and she was unconscious. Rikoh stood over her, an injection pen in one hand, and her jacket in the other.

***

The sudden onslaught of rain meant that Simon and Chris had to catch a cab to get to Andre's warehouse. Stopping outside, Simon paid the fare and joined Chris, who had run off to take shelter beneath an awning next to the building. The place was swarming with police who had raided the FleshFaire just a few hours ago. Chris sneaked Simon in through a side door that was completely unguarded. Once inside, they saw people securing the different displays in the gallery, prepping each to be transported. They moved unnoticed among the crowd of people and made their way quickly to the stairwell.

Chris was honest with Simon. "I have to go collect some things from my office down the hall before they take everything." She looked up the stairwell. "Besides," she said, tears welling up in her eyes, "I don't think I can stand to go up there…"

Simon nodded.

"Be careful," he told her. They shared a brief kiss, and Chris turned, walked out of the stairwell, and disappeared down the hall. Simon continued upstairs and saw Riley standing just outside Andre's office.

"Sonuvabitch…How'd you manage to get up here, Sy? Huh…eh, what does it matter? Youse always been a good dick," Riley said.

"Hey, Mark." Simon walked over but was stopped dead in his tracks when he looked inside the office. There he saw the body of Andre Danam, the man who emceed the FleshFaire—Christine's brother—sitting in a chair facing the door. His eyes had been removed, leaving only dark-red, blood-filled sockets; his throat had been slit. His head was tilted back to make the neck wound seem bigger than it was. He looked like a grim, distorted marionette.

"Shame, huh?" said Riley. "Yeah, we just tracky-wackied that body found over at Manna yesterday to dis guy. Name's Andre Danam. I guess he was pretty big in the FleshArt world. Anyways, we got wind that he was hosting an illegal 'FleshFaire' tonight and we came down to break it up. We've been here a few hours, but it wasn't until half hour ago that someone found a false wall leading up to this room. I tells ya, Sy, there's something bigger going on here. I haven't seen nothin' in months, and now three stiffs in two days. We're looking for Rikoh now and the stiff's sis, a chick called Christine, to figure out just what the fuck's going on!"

"I'm not sure, Mark," Simon said. "But I think there's more at stake here than what either of us first thought."

\*\*\*

Downstairs, Chris had slipped through a hidden panel in the ladies' room that led her to a crawl space just above her office. Moving a grate, she climbed down a service ladder that led to the building's basement. Light broke in through boards in the window, but other than that, it was completely dark. The occasional flash of lightning gave just enough illumination to see the outline of a hatch. She spun the rotating lever that kept the heavy door sealed and pulled it open. Closing the hatch door behind her, she touched the wall, and soft, overhead lighting illuminated her office. It was small room, only half the size of Andre's office, but it was her sanctuary…her safe place. Now that Andre was gone, she wasn't sure how things would work for her. But she knew that it was only a matter of time before the police, or someone else, found this room.

Sitting in a chair at the small desk, she activated the computer terminal. She only kept a few files here, and she moved them to a portable storage cube—a tiny crystalline box that sat next to the terminal and wirelessly stored untold reams of information. The color of the box indicated its status. Right now, it was glowing red, which meant the files she was removing from the system had no other copies. She opened the top drawer of the desk and loaded the contents, six ampuls of IT and two injection pens, into her backpack.

Chris's phone buzzed. It was a text message from Simon. COPS LOOKING FOR YOU. BE SAFE.

She texted back: FINISHING UP. WILL MEET BACK AT YOUR PLACE. XOX

Chris knew that if the cops were after her, they would eventually stumble onto her apartment, so she had to make sure to leave enough time to pick up a few essentials. Her file transfer completed, she looked at the folder underneath hers—the one marked with the letter *A*. She knew she should leave Andre's files alone, but he was gone now, and she had no idea where to start picking up her life again. She opened the folder and found his contact book, which she copied onto the cube. She also found a folder titled CCE. Chris opened this folder, and the window at the top expanded to read, "Chris in Case of an Emergency." It was password protected.

Chris thought for a while. "What would Andre use as a password? Something he would know I'd think of."

It took her a moment, but when she thought of it, she wondered how she even forgot. She typed in the name of her father, and Andre's: James. A simple password, but seeing as their system was not connected to any network, Andre must have felt that it was secure enough.

Three files appeared. One was a letter from Andre to Chris. It had been updated only two days earlier. The other two were electronic key files to access private bank accounts. She opened the text document, which was simply titled, "To my darling Christine," and wept as she read her brother's final words.

*** 

Simon had just received Chris's reply to his text message when he noticed that he had one missed voice message. It was from Rosalee Sanchez:

"Sorry to bother you so late, Mr. Topaz, but I just wanted to let you know that I just got a call from Rikoh with a really weird message. I'm sure it's nothing, but he wants me to come down and meet an investor tonight—right now, actually—and I just have a weird feeling. Detective Riley sent some men to watch over me. Anyway, I wanted to thank you for that, and I'm hoping this *whole* thing is all just a big misunderstanding. If you could return my call when you get this message…I just…um…I'd be glad to hear from you. Have a great night and call me back when you can. Thanks, Simon."

"Shit," Simon thought. "This is *not* good."

He tried to call her personal phone and her apartment, but got no answer. Riley came over and tapped him on the shoulder.

"Youse gotta second? You're gonna want to see this," said Riley.

"I'll be right there," Simon said, trying to dial the office number at the Manna Gallery. It was a long shot, but she might just be there. The call was picked up after two rings, but it was a man's voice.

"Yes?" the man asked.

"Hi, yes, I need to speak with Rosalee

Sanchez. Is she available?" Simon asked.

"Who, may I ask, is calling?"

"Simon Topaz."

The man laughed. "Mr. Topaz, it's wonderful to finally speak to you in person. I've been waiting for this opportunity for quite a while."

"Who is this? Rikoh?"

"No. I'm sorry, but Rikoh has another engagement at the moment. Listen well, Simon Topaz, because I will only tell you this once. If you value the lives of either Miss Sanchez *or* Miss Danam, you will come alone and you will come at once to the Manna Gallery."

The call ended.

Dazed and bewildered, Simon realized there was only one person he could trust right now, even though he didn't want to trust him: Riley. He found Mark sitting at a terminal screen with what appeared to be camera footage of Andre's office.

"There ya is, Sy!"

"Mark! I need your help right away!"

Before Simon could say any more, he saw the footage playing back on the screen. It showed Andre walking into the office, going to confront the man from the FleshFaire, the man in the red scrubs, Dr. D, who was no longer wearing a mask. He was sitting in the chair where Andre's body was found. As soon as Andre entered the room, Rikoh appeared from behind him and stabbed him in the neck with a shiny metal object, what almost looked to be an injection pen. Andre collapsed to the floor, and both Rikoh and the surgeon picked up his body and put it in the chair.

Simon noticed that Andre's eyes were still moving, but the rest of his body was as limp as a rag doll.

Riley and Simon watched as Rikoh handed the surgeon a large knife. Andre was awake and conscious when the surgeon cut out Andre's tongue. The surgeon set the knife down and stood over Andre, watching Andre's eyes moving back and forth—apparently the only parts of his body that he could move. Dr. D then pulled both of Andre's eyes out with his bare fingers, as if he were plucking grapes from their stems. Andre's body was convulsing as a river of blood flowed out of his mouth, and the blood from where his eyes should have been ran in streams down the sides of his face. Andre's gory weeping ended when Rikoh picked up the knife and slashed his throat.

Simon's sense of urgency was almost overwhelming.

"Mark, you should hear this message. Rosalee Sanchez left it for me about four hours ago, and I completely missed it until just now."

Simon played the message for Riley. Pulling out his own phone, Riley called dispatch at the police station. "I need you to patch me through to Keaton and McKenna."

Simon was frantic. He sneaked out of the room and called Chris.

"Stay at your place until you hear from me, okay? Mine's not safe."

From the background noise, he could tell that Chris had already left the warehouse. She was scared. "What the fuck is going on, Sy?"

"I'm not sure. I just know that…"

"What, Sy? Know what?"

"Rikoh killed Andre."

There was a long pause before he heard Chris's voice again. "Sy, whatever happens, please know...I love you." She was crying but managed to say, "I love you, Sy, okay? I love you."

The line went dead.

"Chris? Chris? *Chris*!"

Simon looked at the screen: CALL ENDED. He tried frantically to call her back, but there was no answer.

# THIRTEEN

To my darling Christine:

     If you're reading this, my love, then chances are that something has happened to me. Perhaps I am sitting in a prison cell, or maybe I've left you to fend for yourself in this crazy mixed-up world. Whatever the situation is, please forgive me. I wish I had been a better brother, a better friend, and really…I wished I had been a better human being. More for your sake than for mine. You are truly innocent. You always have been and always will be my rock, my beacon of light, and my will to live.

     Please know that I never meant for anything to happen that would either take me away from you or worse, leave you in a position to have to fight for yourself. You're a survivor, and the fact that you found this letter is proof that you'll find a way. You've always found a way.

     Well, I hope to leave you with some tools to give you an advantage and enough money to live your life however you want to. In this same file folder are two electronic keys: one is for a bank account under the name Danielle Westburg; the other is a safe deposit box at the same bank and under the same name.

Inside the safe deposit box are all the documents you'll need to start life over again: a birth certificate, a new identity chip (which I trust you'll find a way to exchange for the old one), keys to a car sitting parked outside the empty building next to the bank, and other relevant travel and identification materials you'll need to truly become Miss Westburg. The bank account has my entire life's collection of credits. It has enough to meet your needs, wants, and desires for the rest of your life.

There's one more thing I can offer to you, something to escape the life of misery and woe you know now. Here is the address of Dr. Brian Douglas:

2201 E. Oak Street
CS214,
Mainland, New Eden

Dr. Douglas is our guest surgeon for upcoming faires. I've met with him more than a few times, he's Rikoh's boss, and I won't lie—they both make me nervous. But their money is good, and Dr. Douglas has something I think you can use. He has developed a cure for IT…an "antidote," if you will. I was skeptical at first, but then I watched it work. It *does* work, Chris! You no longer have to be a slave to that damnable drug anymore, my love. Dr. Douglas has assured me that he kept an active sample for you, in exchange for a special performance of the Faire. It seems Dr. Douglas has a long-lost nephew he's been trying to reunite with, a man called Simon Topaz. From what I understand, this Mr. Topaz is a private detective who lives and works off the coast.

I should probably tell you also that I know you have been getting IT from Rikoh. You are a grown woman and can manage your life the way you want, but this Rikoh makes me *very* nervous, Chris. I've warned him before that if he ever does anything or *tries* to do anything to you, his punishment will be swift and brutal.

With Dr. Douglas's remedy, I think you can kick this habit once and for all. I believe you have the strength of will and character, and you'll always have my undying love. So please, see Dr. Douglas as soon as possible—for your sake and to get that creep Rikoh from holding this sword of Damocles over your head.

Finally, let me just tell you once again what you have meant to me. I'm sorry I could not give you a better life after dad died, but you must know I love you more than anyone or anything in this world. Please, Chris…or should I say Dani, eh? Please let me provide you with the life I never could while I was by your side. I'm not sure if we have souls, but if we do, mine will always be yours, my dearest sister. I love you.

—A.

# FOURTEEN

Detectives Cyril Keaton and Bill McKenna had been waiting outside the house of a Dr. Brian Douglas, keeping alert to anything that seemed suspicious and trying to keep tabs on their client—a Miss Rosalee Sanchez. The heavy rain was interfering, however, and if it weren't for the Radio Frequency ID chip implanted in Riley's business card, they couldn't even be sure she was still in the house. Suddenly, a call came across on the radio: 2112, PLEASE ACKNOWLEDGE. I HAVE DETECTIVE RILEY READY TO PATCH THROUGH.

Both officers raised their eyebrows, and they looked at one another. "This is damned peculiar," they were both thinking. It wasn't so odd that Riley was calling, but it was strange that he would do it in as early in the morning, as he was doing now.

Keaton touched the large, call/respond button on the screen. "Car 2112 here. Keaton speaking. Go ahead."

"Hey, guys," a gruff voice said. "I know you're keeping a good eye on Miss Sanchez, but I wanted to forward some info along. We have proof her bidness partner is involved in some nasty-wasty shit. Particularly the death of another art dealer, a guy called Andre Danam." Andre's picture appeared on screen, and McKenna pushed a button to make a hard copy printout from beneath the screen. "I needs youse guys to keep an eye out for a Rikoh and a Dr. Brian Douglas. If the moment seems righty-tighty, go ahead and pick Rikoh up on a first-degree murder charge. He's be a slick one, this Rikoh, so if he wants to talk, let him, but otherwise just get him back to the station. As far as Douglas goes, just bring him in as a potential witness, but no formal charge. This doctor is well connected, and I don't want him getting all suspicious just yet. I'm sending you their info now. Good luck, guys, and don't hesitate to call in for backup if shit seems wonky."

Both men checked their service weapons and bundled up in their jackets to brave the rain and cold wind they knew they would face getting into the house. They got out of the car and made their way as quietly and stealthily as they could toward the gate through which Sanchez had entered a few moments prior. With their backs against the fence, both men creeped along the outside, careful to avoid the lockbox, which surely had a camera in it. They edged nearer the gate to find it propped open with a rock. There were no signs that the gate had been forced or manipulated in any way, so Bill McKenna, weapon drawn, ran quickly inside to hold it open. As he did, Cyril Keaton ran past him toward the house. Both men checked the perimeter, and it appeared that all was clear. Positioning themselves on either side of the door to the house, Bill started to knock, only to realize that the door was already open.

He pushed the door open without revealing

himself.

"Police!" he yelled as he ducked inside, his weapon drawn. There was no one in the darkness of the kitchen. Cyril walked in behind him, nervous as hell. Both men slowly made their way through the kitchen, heading toward the light emanating from the living room. A sudden flash of lightning cast a shadow of the figure that stood behind the officers, but they both saw it too late. They heard the muffled sounds of a few compressed-air thuds, and they felt the instant burns in their backs. But by the time the large red pools formed on their shirts, Bill and Cyril's lifeless bodies had fallen forward onto the kitchen floor.

\*\*\*

Chris's taxi pulled up outside the residence of Dr. Brian Douglas. Simon had told her that Rikoh was responsible for Andre's death, but she knew this was only partially true. She had access to the same security footage Simon had seen, and she knew the whole story: although it was Rikoh's cut that finally ended Andre's life, it was Brian who had taken such delight in torturing Andre. Either way, both men would pay dearly for what they did to her brother. That was why she was here now, outside the doctor's house, a gun in the waistband of her jeans, hidden by her jacket.

Making her way quietly up the driveway, trying to hide in the shadows as much she could, Chris was surprised to find the gate slightly ajar. She wasn't sure what she was walking into, which kept her instincts on edge and her head on a swivel. Now standing in the dry beneath the awning, she noticed that the door of the house was also unlocked. She pushed it open, stepped in, and saw two men, both of whom were dressed in suits and jackets, lying facedown in their own blood. Chris reached behind her back to pull the gun from her waistband, never seeing Rikoh, who was standing behind her, his presence blocked by the open door.

Rikoh lunged forward, startling Chris and catching her off guard. With his full weight in motion, he pushed her forward into a counter in the middle of the kitchen. Pain rolled up from her stomach as her breath left her and she felt a rib snap. In a flash, Rikoh had one of her arms pinned behind her back; his hand was on the back of her neck. She struggled to lean back and tried to put the heel of her boot down hard on his toes, but his foot slipped out from behind hers. He drove his knee into her tailbone and swept her leg from beneath her, dropping down on top of her. She hit the ground, her arm taking the load of both their bodies, and with a loud snap, her forearm broke. Chris tried to scream in pain, but nothing was leaving her body. In fact, she began to realize that she couldn't move at all. The pain of her arm breaking had overwhelmed the prick of the injection pen that released its contents into her neck.

The pain in her arm and rib quickly faded under the effect of IT, but her body was paralyzed. The only things she could move were her eyes. Rikoh lifted up her jacket and pulled the gun from her waistband. He put it on the table quite a distance away from both of them and walked back to her prone body. Rolling her over onto her back, he put his hand behind her neck and lifted her face close to his.

"You have no idea how long I've watched you…how long I've waited for this moment. I know you can hear me, you fucking whore. It's a special formulation. You see, Christine, you're my reward for a job well done."

Rikoh pulled a knife from his pocket and dragged the blade along her face, not deep enough to cut, but enough to leave a red imprint before it faded. He continued to speak to her in a low, angry voice.

"We're going to have fun, you and I." Rikoh let out a low chuckle and pressed the point of the knife against her throat. Tears began streaming from the sides of her eyes. Rikoh was confused, she wasn't supposed to be able to cry or even move her eyes as much as she had. It was of no consequence, however. The key thing was that she would not be able to move her body, at least for the next few hours. Rikoh had measured the dose precisely so that she would be coherent enough to know what was happening around her.

Rikoh leaned in and kissed Chris, feeling a shallow breath push through a limp and lifeless mouth. He opened his eyes and could see the horror and disgust in hers. He drew a shallow line with his blade on her left cheek and proceeded to lick the small dribble of blood and tears that mingled there. He laid her head gently on the floor, got up, and closed the door. Rikoh pressed a sequence of keys on the touch screen near the door. Metal shades descended outside each of the windows, stifling the sounds of the rain and the door locks engaging throughout the house.

Chris realized that whatever Rikoh was planning to do, he certainly didn't expect any more visitors.

\*\*\*

The security windows were shuttered outside the Manna Gallery, which, given the heavy rain, hail, and high winds, was not an unusual measure. Simon knew better, though. The man with the resonant voice he had spoken to an hour or so earlier was expecting him to be here alone…which he was. He was unnerved by the threats the man had made against Rosalee and, especially, Christine. He was sure that the man wasn't Rikoh, but with the carnage and mayhem both men left behind them, he also knew they were serious in their resolve, no matter how ambiguous their motive still was. Simon wasn't sure what to expect when he approached the door, but he was not surprised to find it open.

As soon as he entered, the door locked behind him, and the lights in the floor went dark, except for a path, two panels wide, that cascaded into a road of red lights before him. It was a not-so-subtle indicator of where his host wished him to go. Simon pulled a revolver from its side-mounted holster and walked the path slowly, alert for any sound or shadow of a figure that might try to ambush him from the darkness. Although there were partitions between the exhibits, there was no sign of movement. There was only the light at the end of the path. It emanated from a doorway beyond the offices that Simon had visited in the past few days.

When he drew closer, he saw

something…someone…he hadn't seen in years. It was his Anne, but it wasn't her—it was her body dissected from itself. Each of her limbs and her head, torso, and pelvis floated in a clear plastic case, suspended and bolted together as a caricature of a dissected body.

Simon could not stop the overflow of emotion that flooded forth. Anger and sorrow, rage and torment, even though he was numb to the core with the extra surge of IT he had taken, nothing prepared him for the complete ache and shock that consumed the very essence of his body. For so long he had wondered what had happened to her, and not knowing—or worse, thinking he was somehow responsible for her death—was more punishing than any pain or torture his flesh may have endured. This pain cut straight through to his soul. He fell to his knees, freely weeping; the revolver dropped from his hand. Simon felt the presence of a man standing at his side.

"She was and will always be beautiful, Simon…and you should know that she loved you very much, more than she loved anyone else. More than her own family, even."

The man crouched at Simon's side, and Simon suddenly felt a pinprick in the side of his neck. Before he could move, Simon collapsed to the floor. His willed his body to make some gesture, but it was to no avail. The only things that seemed to be working were his eyes and ears. Simon saw a pair of finely polished loafers standing in front of him, and he heard the man's ominous statement: "Don't worry, Simon.

You'll be with your darling Anne again soon enough." Simon heard the words echo, and then suddenly, everything went black.

# FIFTEEN

Chris came to, finding herself strapped to a chair, her wrists and ankles bound to the legs of the chair. Her clothes had been removed except for her bra and panties. A chain lay across her waist and connected to the back of the chair, which, itself was bolted to the wall. Her broken arm had been wrapped in a makeshift splint. Her head and shoulders were free to move, but that was of little use. The gag in her mouth was cinched tightly behind her head.

Looking around the room, she could see the layout of a well-lit and sterile white operating room. There was table in the middle of the room with a headrest on one end and a drain on the other. It looked like an autopsy table. On that table was an unconscious, nude woman, with dark skin and bulbous, fake breasts. She was held down by restraints. To Chris's left was an open door from which music wafted, and to her right was what looked to be a small, dank cage. The smell of rotting meat flowed into her nose and made her want to vomit, but she somehow stifled the urge. She could not see much of the interior of the dark room, but she had a feeling something awful had happened there.

A tall figure, clothed in a red bodysuit with

green gloves and spats, and a black rubber apron, exited the left-hand room of music and light—heaven, Chris had named it in her head—and was walking to the right-hand room of stench and darkness, or hell, as Chris thought of it. Focused on what he was doing, the man did not seem to notice her or the woman on the table. He was carrying a large meat hook, and he disappeared into the darkness of hell. Chris heard the jostling of chains, followed by a thud, as if something large had landed on the floor. It also sounded like a light splash of liquid and then the sudden thwack of the hook being imbedded in a slab of meat. Her horrors were confirmed when she watched the tall man drag a dead, eviscerated, female body into the operating room. The stench from this woman's carcass, which had been rotting for quite some time, was worse than anything Chris could imagine in her wildest dreams. She tried to breathe shallowly and hold her breath for as long as she could at times.

Chris helplessly watched as the tall man pulled the carcass by a hook deeply implanted in its neck. Apart from the facial features that were obviously feminine, there was little left of the body that indicated who or what it once was. All of the flesh and muscle had been stripped away from the upper thighs to just below the knees of both legs. The figure had breasts, but both nipples had been cut away with surgical precision. A long gash ran from the anus to the naval, making use of the natural opening of the vagina, and the body was stretched open. Chris could see that the lower female organs and much of the intestine were missing. The corpse was well preserved, and much of the blood and gristle had been cauterized so as to leave no mess.

Chris watched the tall man drag the body to a marked place on the floor. He pressed the edge of a small panel in the wall, and a hidden door lifted out and swung up on pneumatic hinges. Just inside, from what Chris could see, was a sealed steel door, which the tall man pulled open by unhooking a heavy latch. He rolled a steel cart out. The cart had a flat tray mounted on top, elevated no more than a foot from the floor, and its wheels ran on tracks that nestled inside each other to keep the system clean and compact. Pulling the hook out of the neck of the carcass, the tall man took the body and placed it on the table, folding its arms and feet inward, on top of its trunk. With force and without reverence or ceremony, he slammed the cart back into the cabinet from which it had come. Chris could just see into the small window on the sealed steel door. The tall man walked over to a counter by the sink and pressed buttons on what Chris assumed to be a flat keyboard. With a sudden series of clicks and then the dull roar of flames raging from gas burners, the outer door descended and fit snugly back into its place. To her horror, she realized the chamber was a furnace.

The tall man removed his apron and hung it on a peg in the wall. He then discarded his green gloves, pulling one off from the edge, and then wadding the glove up in the palm of his other hand. He slid open a small door in the counter, which must have led into the oven, and dropped the gloves in, incinerating them. The man paid no attention to Chris, who sat as still and quiet as she could, bound in her chair, or to the young, attractive, nude, woman who lay on the table right behind him. Instead, he walked back nonchalantly into heaven, the room from which soft, warm light and sedate, classical music escaped.

Chris knew she was in trouble and needed to think of something quickly if there was any chance she could live through this. She struggled against the chair and managed to gain a tiny bit of slack where her wrists were tied. It wasn't until she pulled against the legs of the chair that she noticed that the bolt holding the wooden slat to the tubular steel on the left leg was actually quite loose. She heaved against it with all the strength her left leg could muster. Each time she pulled, she felt the binding weaken, and the bolt seemed to slip out that much further, but it also made a loud rattle of metal against metal. She stopped, and her heart skipped a beat, every time she saw the tall man's shadow cross the threshold. When she sensed that he was walking back into the room, she stopped struggling against the chair and pretended to be passed out.

Chris peeked with one eye. The tall man was still wearing the thin, red bodysuit, but this time, there was no mask or cowl to hide his identity. It was Rikoh. He was wearing a new set of red surgical gloves and whistling along to the music playing in heaven: Grieg's "In the Hall of the Mountain King." He walked over to the nude, unconscious woman on the table but spoke into the air while affixing an IV to her arm.

"I suspect why you are here. At first, I wanted to believe it was something your brother may had told you about a cure for IT, but for you to bring a gun…well, that's not very nice, is it? I don't know if you intended to rob or kill us, but both matters now are…inconsequential."

The IV was fixed, and a saline solution began to run slowly into the vein of Rosalee's arm. Rikoh pulled a cart with multicolored syringes close to the table and removed one that was filled with a bright-yellow liquid. He held it up in the air and faced Chris.

"You see, my darling Christine, *this* is the key to your salvation." Rikoh chuckled. "Or, perhaps, to your damnation?" He pondered his own question, looking at the syringe, turning it slowly in his hand.

Chris kept her head down, pretending she was still unconscious.

"Enough with the charade, my Christine," he said. "We both know you are awake, and although your game of possum is cute, it *is* time to get down to business."

Rikoh screwed the syringe into the IV and began to press down on the plunger. He continued to talk while measuring the amount of solution he was pushing into the vein of the bound woman on the table.

"I believe you may already know Miss Sanchez. I have delivered a dose of R-type IT into her bloodstream. Over the next hour, she will not only become fully conscious, but she will feel better than she ever has…that is, until the second phase starts to kick in."

Rikoh walked over to Chris and held her head up. She gave up pretending she was passed out and looked at him. He removed her gag but told her that screaming was quite pointless, as they were isolated from the rest of the world, the two of them. Chris knew that Rikoh was a cold-blooded bastard. She also knew he had no reason to lie. Rikoh knelt down beside her and tossed the gag behind her. He held her head in both of his hands to make sure she was looking directly at him as he spoke. His voice took a softer, almost sympathetic tone.

"You should know, my love, that it wasn't supposed to be this way. If he hadn't been so damned nosy and aggressive, Andre would still be alive. This…all of this…was meant for Topaz. It always was. It seems, however, that too many people know too much. Oh well. Even best-laid plans have their faults."

Chris stared Rikoh in the eye. "I don't know what it is you *think* we know. All I *am* sure of is that you killed my brother, you sick fuck!"

Chris spat in Rikoh's face.

Rikoh smirked, standing up and wiping the spittle from his face. He chuckled.

"Oh, my naive Christine. Even now, you don't understand. I didn't kill him. No, I saved your brother. I saved him from mine. Brian tends to be a bit…theatrical…and his constant waxing nostalgic is more than most twins would be comfortable indulging. But we are two of a kind."

"I have no fucking idea what you're talking about," Chris said.

"How old would you say I am?" Rikoh asked.

Chris shook her head.

"In this body, I am forty-two years old. The cells in my brain, however, have lasted for over four hundred years. I am a child of Genesis, before there was such a thing. I am the living embodiment of Brian Blithe...well, part of him anyway. My brother took his name, knowing that the sole commitment of his life, pardon the pun, would be propagating a new species of predator...of keeping natural selection a part of our commitment to humanity."

"Commitment to humanity?" Chris said, mocking him. "You think murder is a commitment to humanity?"

"Of course it is!" Rikoh exclaimed. "We keep balance in a population that would otherwise run rampant with the extremes of poverty and decadence. Without our level of checks and balances, mankind would run out of control."

Rosalee started to stir against the straps holding her down. Rikoh took notice and walked over to the autopsy table.

"You think IT was only a drug...a painkiller, anesthetic, and euphoric mixed in one. Something to take the edge off. Something to make one's mundane life worth living. But ironically, that's only a side effect. IT is so much more than that, and now that we've got the right concentrations set for different effects of IT and the antidote, R-type, IT is now the single most powerful drug in human history. A single drug to replace all others. With just the right concentration of R-type, which I've given to Rosalee, a person will experience the most exquisite death possible. Rosalee will literally die from a poisoning rush of serotonin and dopamine. Think of it as being on the edge of a giant orgasm when suddenly, all activity in your central nervous system ceases. The body has the equivalent of an electrical blackout, but there is no pain. The last thing she'll remember is the warm flush of pleasure rippling through her body."

Chris was panicked as she saw Rosalee start to flex and moan, her nipples getting harder, and a pool of wetness gathering between her legs. Chris tried again to pull against the chair she was bound to. Clenching her hand into a fist and forcing her fingers to slide beneath her wrist, she twisted at the rope that held her arms bound. She felt a sudden pop on the left leg of her chair. Chris was frightened the sound would get Rikoh's attention, but he was too focused on watching Rosalee. Chris knew she had but one chance. She started crying.

"Now, now. I would have expected more apathy from you, Christine," Rikoh said, turning again toward Chris.

"Please don't..." Chris sobbed. "She doesn't need to die too. Just...just take what you want from me."

Rikoh let out a maniacal laugh.

"Don't worry. I plan to. You should also know, however, there is no known way to reverse the effect of R-type. So as sympathetic as I am to your cause, there is no way for me to stop the process now...even if I wanted to."

"What about another dose of IT? Could that counter the effects?" Chris pleaded.

Rikoh flashed a soulless grin. "It just might...but you would have to persuade me."

Chris bowed her head. "Whatever it takes. Just, please...no more death."

Rikoh loaded a syringe of green-glowing IT into the IV line. Before he pushed the plunger down, however, he carefully laid the syringe on the table. He walked over to Chris, and with one hand, pulled her hair back, while unzipping his red jumpsuit with the other. He pulled out his large erection and pushed it toward her face. Chris resisted, turning her head away from his dick until he pull harder on her hair.

"Uh, uh, uh…come on, now. The nicer you are to me, the nicer I'll be to Rosalee, here."

Chris knew he was right, and if she managed this correctly, she really only had one shot. She opened her mouth, and Rikoh slammed his cock to the back of her throat, holding her head close until she gagged. He was using one hand to steady himself; the other was pressed against the back of her head. He too busy and focused on the pleasure of the blow job that he never noticed that Chris had slipped her left leg free from the chair leg. Her ankle was still tied to the wooden slat with the carriage bolt attached, but the slat now swung freely. She waited until Rikoh tried to hold her head close, and then she made her move. With nearly his entire dick in her mouth, she slammed her teeth shut as hard as she could. Gnawing and tearing, she felt her teeth cut through the soft flesh and spongy material as blood gushed into her mouth. In the same instant, she lifted her leg and slammed the bolt as hard as she possibly could into the back of Rikoh's ankle. She did it repeatedly. She could feel his Achilles tendon sever after the third strike, which caused Rikoh to crumple into a bloody, screaming heap on the ground by her feet. Chris was able to pull her fingers completely underneath her hand, and with a quick twist of her wrist, her arm was free.

Spitting out what remained of his dick and the blood in her mouth, Chris was able to untie herself from the chair. Using the blood-covered bolt in the wooden slat, she pried at a rusty link in the chain around her waist. With no little amount of force and serendipitous fate, the link busted open, and she was freed from the chair. Her mind was awhirl with what to do next when she spotted a syringe of IT on the cart. She screwed a hypodermic needle onto the end and ran back over to Rikoh's bloody, battered body on the ground.

"Here," she said in a mocking tone. "This should help!"

Chris rammed the needle into his chest and pressed down as hard as she could on the plunger. He grew motionless, and his pupils widened. She could tell he was still breathing, but with the dose of IT she gave him, he was completely paralyzed—trapped in his own body. She could figure out to do with him later; for now, he was locked in perpetual agony.

Chris rushed over and pushed the plunger of the IT syringe hooked into Rosalee's IV. The waves of pleasure that rolled across Rosalee's face began to subside, and she became lucid and noticed not only that she was naked but also that she was tied down to the table.

"Wha...what the *fuck* is happening?" Rosalee screamed as she began to cry.

"It's okay...sh...it's okay. I'm here to help you," Chris reassured her as she started undoing the straps that held Rosalee down. Rosalee sat up and hugged Chris as tightly as she could. Chris helped Rosalee off the table and kept her upright as her legs started to buckle beneath her. Both women hobbled into the ornate office, the door to which had been left open by Rikoh.

Just to the right-hand side of the door were two chairs. One was empty, and the other held a stack of clothes neatly folded. Sorting through them quickly, Chris recognized her clothes and assumed, correctly, that the others must be Rosalee's. Both women dressed quickly.

"Where's Rikoh?" Rosalee asked.

"Don't worry; he can't hurt us anymore. Quick, try to find a phone and call the cops," said Chris. "I've got to find Simon!"

"Topaz?" Rosalee asked.

Chris nodded vigorously.

"He's at Manna with Brian. I overheard Rikoh talking to him…something about a family reunion."

Chris turned to leave the room. Rosalee stopped her by jumping in front of her and hugging her again. "Thank you," she said, looking Chris in the eye. Then suddenly, she kissed Chris on the lips. Chris gently pushed Rosalee away.

"I was never here," said Chris. "Seal the door in case anyone tries to get in."

Rosalee nodded.

"Be careful," she said.

Chris walked out of heaven, and Rosalee closed the door behind her. Chris was alone in the bleak operating theater, aside from Rikoh's pathetic carcass lying motionless in a heap on the floor. Blood continued to pour out from between his legs, and Chris went to the sink to wash his blood from her hands and face. Next to the sink, she saw the screen that Rikoh had left open, showing the controls for the incinerator. She had an idea. She pushed the buttons to open the door and extend the flat tray on which Rikoh had put the other body. There was nothing left on it now but a pile of ash. Chris dragged Rikoh over and pulled him onto the tray. Looking at the counter, she spotted another syringe with the yellow R-type drug. She pushed the cart bearing Rikoh's bleeding, battered body into the incinerator. Before closing the door, she felt for Rikoh's femoral artery and pushed the hypodermic needle loaded with R-type into his leg. Quickly shutting and latching the door, she could hear his muffled screams as he thrashed inside his fiery tomb.

Chris pressed the green "on" button and watched as the timer counted down from ten seconds. She crossed the room and found the panel that opened the doorway to the stairwell. As she stepped out of the room, she heard the burners click on and Rikoh's muffled screams, until there was silence.

As Chris ascended the stairs, tears welled up in her eyes, and only one thought came to mind: "That's for Andre, you miserable fuck!"

# SIXTEEN

Bright flashes of white light caught Simon's attention enough to make him want to open his eyes. He was unsure about just how long he had been unconscious, and his mind was in a million different places. Simon wasn't even sure where he was or if any of the horrible images that kept appearing in his mind's eye were real or just scenes from a nightmare. His eyes focused on the hazy forms of two people in the room: one, a man standing before him, dressed in red scrubs; the other, a woman…Simon's woman…Anne. But she wasn't standing. If anything, she was floating. Pieces of her body floated and hovered in a balanced, suspended animation, all in containers of different sizes and shapes. In a few short moments, all of Simon's greatest fears were confirmed. He no longer had to speculate on Anne's fate. But who would do such a thing to her, putting her on display like this? How did she die? Did she suffer, or was she already dead when someone decided encase her body in such a grandly morbid way?

Simon's eyes adjusted to the light, and he realized that he was still in Manna Gallery, but he was no longer free to move as he had been. He was bound to a chair, which he only realized when he moved to stand up and felt metal bands around his wrists and ankles. These bands did not directly tie Simon, but an invisible force kept him from moving too far. He realized that he was held in place by magnetic restraints.

"Well, Sy," the man in red scrubs said. "It took a while, but the family is finally together at last."

Simon focused his eyes on the man. He knew he that he saw him clearly, but the face was identical to the one in the Blithe family photo he had seen two days prior.

"Brian…Blithe?" Simon asked in disbelief.

"Ah, no. Brian Douglas. Dr. Brian Douglas—nee Blithe, and I'm sure your mind is asking more questions than it can answer right now," Brian said.

"I don't get any of this…"

Brian pulled a chair over to sit in front of Simon.

"Well, strangely enough, Simon, your whole life has led to this one moment. But I guess that's true of anyone, right? There's nothing we can do to change our pasts, and our futures only exist based on the choices we make now. You're still confused."

Brian relaxed in his chair, while Simon looked on helplessly.

"Humankind is no more an evolved species than most others on this planet. We've adapted and overcome much to get where we are now, but we really are not any more in charge—or, really, even in control—of anything in our own lives, much less this world…or all things in the universe, for that matter. What we have sitting around us are monuments and testimonials to a time when certain men and women realized man's folly in thinking he was the dominant species. All of the artifacts, relics, and reproductions you've seen in this exhibit are personal memories and treasures we've lost in the last four hundred years."

Simon scoffed. "You sound as though you were there...that somehow this is *your* collection."

"Indeed, it is; and indeed, I was."

"But I thought Rikoh..."

Brian sighed. He knew he would have to have patience if Simon was to appreciate how important his role would be in everyone's (especially Brian's) future.

"Well, Sy, it's not *incorrect* to say this is Rikoh's as much as it is mine. You see, Rikoh and I go way back—four hundred and sixty years, to be honest. Rikoh is as much of me as I am of him—and as much as you are to both of us."

Simon was trying to process everything that was happening, but Brian noticed the confusion on his face.

"Simon, we are all brothers: you, Rikoh, and I. More than brothers, really. We are the same."

Simon laughed. "I'm not four hundred years old," he said.

Brian smiled a sinister smile.

"No. *You* are not, but your mother—my sister—was. She was until she got pregnant with you. She was a beautiful woman. You know, you've seen her."

"I never knew my mother," said Simon.

Brian pulled a picture from his pocket and stared at it.

"No. I don't believe you ever did. But you *have* seen this."

Brian revealed the photo to Simon: it was an older, smaller version of the same Blithe family photo Simon had seen locked in the vault a few days earlier. It was the photo of the family picnic.

"I don't understand. You killed them all..."

"Wrong!" Brian shouted. He took a deep breath and composed himself. "I saved them. You know nothing of your ancestry, Simon Topaz!"

Brian arose from his chair and turned his back to Simon, continuing to speak.

"For being such a great detective, you never could find out who your parents were, or even what happened to your beloved Anne?"

Brian pointed at the effigy that was once Simon's beloved.

"If not for me, you would never have seen her again."

Simon was enraged. "But why...why kill her? She was innocent!"

Brian appeared offended by the accusation.

"I did not kill her, Sy. Sindel's men, those cretins, did that. You fucking around with drug dealers and gangsters, Simon, that's what killed her. I preserved her. Every day, we push the boundaries of genetics and molecular biology. The fact that I have been able to survive this long is proof of that. I am *not* immortal, Simon. In fact, far from it. I have only been able to survive as long as I have because of a mutation in our genes. When your mother got pregnant, she began to age quite quickly. Neither of us knew why, until I found my mistake." Brian fought back a tear.

"It was a difficult birth, Sy. Not your fault; you were as perfect as she was. Whatever the combination was that had made her strong for so many years began to fail. She started to suffer, and my formulation of IT was better than any other ever made. She…" Brian looked at Simon with tears in his eyes. "She was taking IT. Not a lot, mind you, but in all the years of making suffering less painful for people, we never once thought to try it on ourselves. We can't feel the way most people do, Sy. There have been people who are meant to suffer: my bastard of a happy-handed, never-satisfied father; my mother, who paraded her family as a portrait of perfection, all the while knowing what dear ol' dad was doing to Emily. They deserved what they got."

"What about the children?" Simon asked. "What did they do that was so bad to suffer the way they did?"

"They were innocents? Like your Anne, here? Let me clue you in on something, Simon. You don't have to live through half a millennium of human history to know that there are *no* innocents."

Simon briefly looked beyond Brian to see a familiar shadow standing behind him. Stalling for time, Simon scoffed. "So, even if I were to believe you, what is this all, then? Just a family reunion with Uncle Bri?"

"You have no idea the power of the blood that runs in your veins, Simon. You may have tainted your life and signed your warrant on mortality, but locked in your DNA is something even I don't have."

"Why not just ask for my help?" Simon asked as he suddenly felt his wrist and ankle cuffs slacken.

"Because of what I've been tasked to do and those who need me to do it. I would let you help if I could, but there is something…bigger. We are all a part of something bigger than you, IT, Leader, or even New Eden itself: me. After hundreds of years and billions of lives, I am finally able to give The Council what they wanted."

"What about Rikoh? He's your family too. Why not just use him?"

"Rikoh is not my family; he's me. Rikoh is a direct clone of my DNA. Actually, he's the fifth generation of me—loyal but expendable. Like many of the Genesis kids."

Brian heard a female voice behind him. "He's not likely to be helping anyone soon."

Brian spun around to see Chris standing a few feet away, holding a gun at his chest.

"What have you done, you *bitch!*" Brian exclaimed.

Brian wasn't aware that as he turned around, Simon had grabbed the injection pen from his jacket pocket and spun the dial fully open. He leapt up and jabbed it into Brian's neck. Brian turned around, instantly realizing what Simon had done. He was only able to take a few steps toward Simon before falling, passed out, to the floor.

Simon rushed over to Chris, who was running to him also. They held each other and kissed until Simon suddenly broke away. "What took you so long?" he asked.

With her hands on his face, she smiled. "Well,

I had some other stuff to attend to." She kissed him again, and they held each other in what seemed like an eternal embrace.

"What now?" Chris asked.

"I'll give you a few to get out of here. Then I'll call Riley. I don't know what will happen to Uncle Brian, here, once the IT wears off, but I don't even want to be close. What about you? I will help for as long as I can, but I can't hide you forever."

Chris stuck the gun in the back waistband of her jeans. "Well, there are some things of Andre's I need to settle. I'll probably be looking for a job after all this, seeing as most of my employers are dead or going to prison. Don't worry about me. I'll see you in a few days."

"Well," said Simon, "I may have a position open. What do you think about solving crimes instead of being an accessory to them…Danielle?" Simon smiled at the look of stunned astonishment on Chris's face.

"How did you know?"

Simon kissed her hand and said simply, "I'm a much better detective than I look."

Chris started to walk away and then she looked back at Simon.

"This isn't over," she said. "We still have quite a bit to discuss."

Simon simply smiled and said, "I love you…whoever you are."

He had to laugh as he saw Chris skip away before she got serious about getting to the back of the building and ducking out of sight.

Simon walked past Brian's form and knelt down. "You and I also have quite a bit to discuss, Uncle Brian. But in due time."

Finally, he walked up to the display of Anne's effigy in glass containers. Tears began to stream down his cheeks as he kissed her face through its glass enclosure. Simon dialed Riley's number on his videophone.

Riley answered in his usual gruff manner. "Sy, I was worried about choo. Whasup?"

"Can you send a heavily armed detail down to Manna Gallery? I found our accomplice in Andre Danam's murder. He's subdued for now, but he will need to be heavily restrained and monitored. Security level A."

"Will doosey-woosey. ETA ten min. Perp's name isn't Brian something, is it?" Riley asked.

"Yeah, Dr. Brian Douglas. Old family friend." Simon chuckled.

"Ah, but youse don't have no family."

"Long-lost relative, it seems. Be here soon, huh Mark?"

Riley smirked. "If there ain't nothin' I've ever been, it's tardy, Sy."

"Oh and Mark, could you send another truck? There's another FleshArt 'thing' here to be wheeled out."

Simon hung up the phone and sat down on the floor next to Anne's tomb. He couldn't hold her anymore, but maybe Brian was right. If she had been preserved properly, there might be another chance for her in the future. All things being equal, though, Simon knew *he* would never see her again.

# SEVENTEEN

Brian awoke to find himself manacled to the inside of a van. Through his fogginess, he saw three cops, one to each side, and one sitting in front of him. His head was pounding, and he was frantically trying to recall what had happened. He remembered being in the gallery and seeing the Danam girl…Then, he felt his neck.

"That bastard must have dosed me!"

Brian was furious, but he was even more worried. He knew what happened to his sister once she took IT, but he had no idea what would happen to him. Being shackled and under arrest didn't help matters much, either. He needed to escape and get back to his house.

"Where are we going?" he asked the guards.

None of them answered. They simply glared at him. His answer came soon enough as he felt the van pull to a stop, and the engine went silent. The door of the van opened wide, and his hope of escape quickly fled his mind as he looked out onto a sea of robotic men. The human guards unlocked his cuffs and pushed Brian to the edge of the van. Stepping out, he knew where he was, but it didn't reassure him of his fate.

"What does *he* want me for?" Brian wondered.

The men stood inside a large white room with no noticeable doors or windows to the outside. It seemed to stretch on forever. Outside the van, surrounded by robotic soldiers, the guards led him to an open clearing in the room and took positions standing around him. In a flash, blue lights shot up from the floor to form a square column surrounding them; he felt the ground shift so subtly that it took a moment to realize they were ascending. The translucent blue hue surrounded them, and he noticed the robotic men growing smaller as the elevator climbed. He wasn't sure if they were still moving until the blue walls descended into the floor, and he realized they were in another room made of gold and sapphire. Ornate tapestries hung from the walls, and the hall was strewn with cushions and pillows of deep colors. Windows opened in the pyramid top above him. It was now day, but the gray and black storm clouds were so thick that everything seemed to be in a perpetual dusk.

Brian walked with the guards past giant golden statues and a line of robotic men that ran the length of the corridor. At the end of the hall was a single chair, in which the men motioned for Brian to sit. When he did, they unlocked his cuffs and walked away, leaving him alone. But he knew he wouldn't be alone for long before His Majesty came to call.

Sitting in the chair, Brian felt the magnetic restraints immediately bind his wrists and ankles. The line of metallic men turned in unison, facing away from him.

"This can't be good," he thought.

Hearing the hum of machines behind him, Brian grew anxious. A long, muted whirl began to drone on as something suddenly hit the rear of the chair. Unable to turn around, Brian didn't know what this was, but soon, two mechanical arms swung into place alongside him. He tried to struggle against the restraints, but his efforts were quickly subdued when he felt something pierce his neck. As the IT glow began to take hold, he hardly noticed that his chair was being raised, and it was morphing into a table, allowing his body to lie flat. Brian was gazing into the stars through the transparent canopy. There were few clouds, and the rain had ceased, but Brian couldn't have cared less. He lay on the table, his mind wrapped in a warm blanket of fog, and his body completely numb.

Brian kept staring at the stars and barely noticed the arrival of the four humanoid robots that now surrounded the table.

"Beautiful," he thought as he tried to make out the constellations. He never felt the line of hoses that pushed through his flesh into his vital organs. From each corner of the table, the humanoid doctors each produced a laser that drew a line bisecting Brian's body. After the beams met and converged into a single solid line, Brian barely felt the pressure as his skin was peeled off his body. The surgeons worked quickly, preserving every muscle and tendon as they methodically removed them from Brian's body. As a needle pierced his cerebellum, Brian only thought of how beautiful the stars were as they slowly faded, and his mind fell into darkness.

\*\*\*

Simon had finished answering all of the questions Riley could throw at him. Neither man could fathom the motive behind what Brian had done, and no matter what questions Riley asked, Simon's account of what happened at the gallery a few hours earlier left him feeling unsteady.

"So youse sure that's all theres is to it?" Riley asked.

"You can watch the surveillance video. We must have had a power glitch or something, because the magnolocks suddenly disengaged, and I was able to subdue this Dr. Douglas when he was distracted."

"And you're sure you don't know what distracted him?"

"I haven't the foggiest," Simon lied. "What did the tape show?"

Riley chuckled.

"Welly-well, that's just it, Sy. Tape dinnit show nuthin'."

"Good girl," Simon thought.

He knew that Chris would have a chance to erase the footage if he stalled long enough, and he was glad she did. Otherwise, he might still be trying to form the story in his head well enough to tell it, or worse, be caught in a lie and implicate her.

"The last time youse saw the Danam girl…"

Simon was getting irritated. "I told you, Mark, it was at the FleshFaire. Christine Danam invited me to meet with her brother, and I tried chasing her down when the police started raiding, but she gave me the slip."

It was a bold lie, for in fact, if it hadn't been for Chris, Simon would be dead right now. There was no way he could let Riley know that.

"Well, if youse do hear from her, lemme know, okay? We found that creep Rikoh's body at the doctor's house with Rosalee Sanchez. She told us about Rikoh trying to assault both dem, her and the Danam girl. Danam apparently sealed her in the office, where we found her. Nowy-wow, I'm not sayings that this Christine chick murdered Rikoh. As far as I know, it was self-defense. But I tells ya, Sy, it's the only lead I've got to go on."

Simon nodded. Whatever suspicions he had about either Rikoh's or Rosalee's fates were answered.

"Is that all?" Simon inquired.

"Yeah…for *nows*. Don't go too far in case I needs ya."

Simon got up from the chair across the desk from Riley. He was walking out of the room when Riley spoke again.

"Just so youse knows…she's down in evidence. In case you wanna talk to her or any things."

Simon never turned around to face Riley.

"Thanks," he said quietly.

Simon walked to the elevator, debating whether to hit the "basement" button. Remembering the IT dream he had a few nights prior gave him a more comfortable feeling about the entire ordeal. In his gut, he knew that Anne not only forgave him, but she approved of him moving on. It was just as he felt when he couldn't find her; after the first year, his sorrow and grief turned to a compulsion to know her fate. If she was indeed dead, then she was at peace. But if she had been preserved, as Brian had told him, perhaps someone could give her a better life sometime in the future. He pushed the button to land on the first floor instead. Simon decided it would be best to return to his office. That would be the best place to wait and see if anyone, no matter what his or her name might be, would show up.

***

Brian's vision was starting to clear. He could make out indistinct shadows of figures that surrounded him, but everything looked as if it were underwater. He was becoming aware, knowing that he must be in some sort of hospital or recovery room. Yet, for as much as he willed it to move, nothing on his body responded the way he hoped. He tried to speak.

"WHERE…WHERE AM I?"

The words formed in his head, but the voice he heard was not his own. In fact, the words he heard weren't even human. It was the sound of a computer-generated voice.

"What the fuck is going on?" he thought.

He recalled being at the gallery with Simon, and the Danam girl screwing things up.

"Good morning, Brian. You have seemed to have gotten yourself into quite the ordeal."

Two men appeared in Brian's fuzzy vision. One was a tall, thin man with sharp features; the other was shorter but much more muscular and toned—a perfect body that had been built and refined over the years for the magnificent Leader of New Eden. It was the hawkish man who was speaking.

"For best-laid plans, you have really fucked this up. With all due respect, sir."

The man was finally standing close enough that Brian could see who he was, although he didn't understand.

"RIKOH?" The voice was that of a machine again.

"Ah," said Leader. "Close, Dr. Douglas. But alas, no. This is Riloh, and he's here to make sure things go…smoother…next time. The Council is not pleased that you would let yourself be jeopardized by a petty personal matter. Your work and your knowledge are *much* too valuable to be trivialized by some junkie detective—even if he *is* your blood."

"WHAT IS HAPPENING?"

"I believe I can answer that, my dear doctor," said Riloh. "You see, when you allowed your body to become tainted with IT, you were no longer immune to the ravishes of time. Your perfect drug does not blend so well with your perfect DNA, it seems. If it wasn't for the fact that you were arrested, giving us the chance to intervene, you would be stuck: a genius brain in a rotting corpse."

Brian was lucid enough to realize why he couldn't move his limbs. He looked down and saw through the haze that he no longer had a body. Not sure exactly what he was, Brian wanted to panic, but he was met with a feeling of calm relief the moment he did.

"WHAT HAVE YOU DONE?"

Leader took it upon himself to answer. "What

we had to. You are without a body right now, Dr. Douglas. It's a problem that will be corrected in a few moments. The IT corrupted most of your tissue, but our surgeons were able to collect just enough raw cellular material to clone you a new body. Per the Council's wishes, you will be given something no one besides me has ever had: a new cloned replica body. We expect you to take care of it this time."

"WHAT MUST I DO?"

"You'll be transplanted here," said Riloh. "Once the operation is complete, you will sent in stasis to Oceania so you may begin recovery. My younger counterpart, Rimoh, and I will help you through the transition. Your body will grow at a natural rate, so we suspect it will take about fifteen years for you to be, well…yourself again."

"We have begun processing a Rinoh clone to help you in the latter stages," Leader said. "Riloh will stay here to assist me, and Rimoh will stay in Oceania. Besides, by the time you're healthy enough to come back to New Eden, the Rinoh unit will be young and agile enough to do the majority of the heavy work."

"I UNDERSTAND."

"I hope you do, Doctor, for your sake. The Council is willing to give you another chance. I'd just as soon let you rot naturally like any lower person should. But it seems that whatever you sold them on, they're buying. What was it, anyway? What is so damned important that I've been asked to go out of my way to make sure you live?"

Leader's anger was starting to seep through his calm demeanor.

"DID THE COUNCIL NOT TELL YOU?"

Leader shook his head.

"THEN, FOR *YOUR* SAKE, SIR, PERHAPS IT WOULD BE BEST TO LEAVE THE MATTER ALONE."

Leader was not pleased by Brian's words or the attitude he had the audacity to show. "If you think for one moment I will be talked down to by—"

"YOU WILL DO WHAT THE COUNCIL ORDERED," Brian interrupted. "YOU WILL DO WHAT THEY SAY, AND IF I AM TO COMPLETE THEIR MISSION, YOU WILL ENSURE THE SAFETY OF SIMON TOPAZ."

Leader was stunned as much as he was angry, but he knew what would happen if he disobeyed a direct order from the Council. Not only would he lose the gift of regeneration, but he would also spend the little life he would have left in a nerve amplifier. The Council would make sure he suffered more than anyone possibly could. If Leader was to have a chance at redeeming himself before the Council and making Brian show him the proper respect, he would need to wait for another time.

"Very well," Leader said, seething. "But know this, Dr. Douglas: one misstep, one bad move, and your, or your family's, meager existence will be the least of your concerns."

"THEN WE ARE AGREED," said Brian's mechanized voice. "RILOH, RESTORE ME TO CRYOSTASIS."

Brian saw Riloh move just out of his field of view before the dark descended. Riloh turned to talk to Leader but saw that he had already exited the room. He stared at what was left of Dr. Brian

Douglas: a simple brain attached to eyes and ears and floating in a liquid suspension. Wires ran from different areas of the brain to an umbilical cord that attached it to a computer.

"Until we meet again, my good doctor."

# EPILOGUE

It had been a week since the incident in the Manna Gallery, and Simon thought most of the dust had settled. When Brian Blithe/Douglas said they were involved in something bigger than anyone could imagine, he really didn't know just how much bigger. Riley kept in touch with Simon, and the whole debacle, as cut-and-dried as it seemed to be, become ever more complicated. Simon could take comfort in some things. Rosalee Sanchez was safe, and though she would need years of therapy to get over what she had seen, she was doing a good job of putting her life back together. In fact, Simon was elated to get tickets to the gala opening of Manna Gallery's newest exhibit, featuring trinkets of twentieth-century mechanization. The note that Rosalee included confirmed that her inspiration for the exhibit was Simon's personal collection, which made him feel good. Even so, he told her that he probably would not make it to the premier, but he promised to stop by when he could.

A voice came over the intercom: "Mr Topaz, a Detective Riley is here to see you."

"Send him in, please."

Riley's sudden appearance, while unexpected,

was not shocking. Simon greeted him as he walked through the door. "Hey, Mark! How's tricks?"

"Well, Sy, I gotta tells ya, there's some weird shit going on with your pal, the doctor."

Simon directed Riley to have a seat and went to the sideboard to pour him a drink. "Really? What's Uncle Bri up to these days? On ice I hope?"

Riley took a sip of his drink, and Simon took a seat behind his desk.

"Well, he's being sent to Oceania," Riley said. "Some special security squad…I dunno, all these orders are coming from Leader himself. Something to do with criminal research, so they want the doc down there, but I gots ta tell ya, Sy, the whole thing stinks."

"If he's under Leader's guard, there shouldn't be any issue. I have a feeling he'll rot in prison soon anyway. The guy is getting up there in age." Simon smiled.

The office door opened, and a beautiful young pixie of a woman entered.

"Sorry to bother you, Mr. Topaz. I have the court documents ready from Manna's insurance company," she said.

"Perfectly okay, Ms. Westburg. In fact, I'd like you to meet an old friend of mine. Detective Mark Riley, meet my new assistant, Danielle Westburg."

Riley shook hands with the dark-haired beauty and cocked an eyebrow at Simon as if to say, "You're doing well for yourself, Simon…"

"So, any luck finding the Danam girl?" Simon asked.

"Nope. You says the last time you saws her

was that night we raided the FleshFaire?" Riley asked.

"I haven't seen or heard from Christine Danam since—"

"Youse be sure to tell me if you do though, right?" Riley looked at both Simon and Danielle and smirked.

"You'll be the first person I call, Mark," Simon said. "Was there anything else? How's Anne?"

"She's been moved to long-term storage at the medical plaza. Doctors there say she's clinically dead, but whatever that stuff they used to preserve her was, it's better than anything they've seen before. Whelp, I better get back to the station. Just wanted to keep you up to snuff."

The men stood, shook hands, and Simon walked Riley to the door.

"Youse hear anything else, lemme know. Okay?" Riley said in a hushed tone. "T'was a pleasure to meet you, Miss Westburg."

"You too, Detective Riley," Danielle said. "I'll probably be seeing more of you in the near future."

"Hopes so," said Riley. "Take care of yourself, Sy."

"You too, Mark."

The men embraced, and Simon shut the door behind him.

Danielle looked at Simon with a smirk, and he grinned. She made sufficient changes her hairstyle and clothing to fool Riley, and the new contacts made her eyes look green.

"I know I'm still getting used to these contacts, but shouldn't they register that you were lying about not seeing Christine Danam?" she asked.

Simon walked over to her and put his arms around her waist. She put her arms around his neck. "Well, it wasn't a lie," Simon said. "The last time I saw Chris was at the gallery when she saved my ass…again. I really started to miss her, but a few days later, I met you, Dani…and everything seemed…well, I should say, I knew that everything would be all right."

Simon and Danielle kissed. It was a ritual they were accustomed to, but it wasn't getting old for either of them. They both suspected that matters with Uncle Brian were far from over, but despite the horrors of their pasts, they were together. And in their eyes, that made the future and everything else, as Simon said, all right.

# APPENDIX

**Notes on Intravenous Transanalgesic Ver 3**
Dictated by: Dr. Brian Douglas, MD, FACS
Date: June 23, 2377, 0400 NEMT

It has taken quite a bit of time and more than a few
test subjects, but I believe I have found the right
chemical sequencing to make IT v3 the most potent
form yet, while still achieving all of the benchmarks I
set with the development of this drug in the first
place. While v2 was sufficient to satisfy the Council's
requirements, it lacked the component to retard aging
that I so desperately need for my dear Emily. When
she delivered our wonderful little Simon, IT v2 was
sufficient to ease the pain of her difficult childbirth,
but it has caused her to age at a dramatic rate. The
deterioration of her cells has sped up substantially,
causing her to age five years for every thirty days, by
my estimate. At the rate her body is decaying, she
will be dead before year's end unless I can find the
right combination to slow down or perhaps even
reverse the cellular-deterioration process. However,
not knowing what in our DNA has allowed us, Em
and me, to live as long as we have, it's nearly
impossible to solve this riddle. I dare not test this or

any other formulation on myself, knowing for certain that I am the only one who shares our unique form of extended mortality. It is not known yet if little Simon carries this gene, as neither Em nor I realized we were aging more slowly than normal until we were in our early twenties, and only then after a decade of social awkwardness.

Simon's birth, itself, is a great mystery. Although the idea of an immaculate conception has been teased since the time of the Christ, I still have not been able to understand how or why Emily's body rejected all seeds but was still able to carry a fetus to full term and deliver a healthy and vibrant child. If the Council ever knew of Emily's ability to have a child without a partner or donor sperm, I'm afraid it would do everything it could to take her away from me. I cannot let that happen, so I had Simon placed in a Genesis Center, even though he is pureborn, so as not to arouse suspicion. I will be keeping track of his progress, and when he reaches his thirtieth birthday, which is the age at which both Em and I seemed to have plateaued, I will make myself known to him. I believe he is the key to the connection between our extended life and where our bloodline progresses from there. I dare not interact with him until then, lest the Council grow suspicious and we lose everything we hoped for in breeding a new human for a new age—as the Council's beloved Genesis Centers, with their random genetic anomolies, has tried to put forth as our new population.

Tonight, I will deliver this dose of v3 to my precious Emily. All of the lab readings and test animals have reacted positively to v3, but there's no way of knowing their mental condition. I fear v3 may have hallucinogenic effects that could popularize it as a recreational drug. If these are not severe, we will just dismiss them as side effects. The drug's real value is not only stopping the aging process but providing a chance to reverse it. Emily is so sick, and I have worked nonstop to make something—anything—work.

*** 

**Notes on Intravenous Transanalgesic Ver 3**
Dictated by: Dr. Brian Douglas, MD, FACS
Date: June 23, 2377, 1604 NEMT

Emily was given a 30cc (25mcg/cc) dose of IT v3 at 1200 hours New Earth Mean Time. The euphoric effects were noted instantly, as well as the drug's ability to block pain signals. At 1400 hours, Emily experienced what she called a living daydream. She was in a catatonic state for close to an hour and described her dream, which I will journal outside this report. She described the vividness and lucidity of the dream as so intense that she felt as if I had somehow made her prescient. This condition was not unexpected, except in the degree of psychocognitive ability it seemed to manifest.

As far as the cessation of cellular deterioration, v3 seems to have slowed the process, but I fear there is nothing to reverse it. By my estimate, my dearest Emily's organs will begin to fail from fatigue within the week.

***

**Notes on Intravenous Transanalgesic Ver 3**

Dictated by: Dr. Brian Douglas, MD, FACS
Date: June 30, 2377, 2112 NEMT

My beloved sister and true companion left her mortal
form at precisely 1111 New Earth Mean Time.

\*\*\*

**Notes on Intravenous Transanalgesic Ver 4**
Dictated by: Dr. Brian Douglas, MD, FACS
Date: December 25, 2380, 0030 NEMT

The Council has taken IT away from me and assigned
it to Dr. Porter Maliki. I know the Council's intent. It
wishes to pepper the streets of every city-state in New
Earth with my antiaging analgesic serum to combat
its failure with Project Genesis. While the project has
been implemented worldwide with specially designed
centers for incubation and education, the Council
knows there is still a dramatic flaw in the "children"
beyond sterility, which, for cloning, is
inconsequential. Without the introduction of IT, the
Genesis "kids" peak at about thirty years of age.
Ironically, that is the direct opposite my experience.
When I was in my thirties, I experienced the biggest
slowdown of the aging/deterioration process.
However, these Genesis "mutants" seem to age
significantly at that point. The Council believes that
by distributing IT, knowing the euphoric effect of the
drug, it can trick the populous into taking the drug,
thus slowing the cellular deterioration to a rate similar
to twentieth-century mortality rates.

However, I put in a fail-safe mechanism. If the
optimum dosage of IT is exceeded, as determined by
body weight, the drug will cause complete paralysis.

The duration of the paralysis can be minutes to years, based on the dosage. With a simple tweak of the formula, what the Council is selling as paradise will become a living nightmare.

***

**Notes on Intravenous Transanalgesic Ver R**
Dictated By: XXXXXXXXXXX
Date: XXXXXXXXXXXXXXXXXXXXXXXXXX

The Council has returned IT to me—whether it meant to or not. My research has been conducted without documentation or restraint. I dare not make notes beyond this, lest the Council tries to circumvent my progress. Already it has meddled too much, and that has cost the world dearly…not that I have any remorse. I am simply making this note on the introduction of R-type in case something happens to me. R-type has proved to be an antagonist to IT. When introduced into the bloodstream, all euphoric and analgesic properties of IT are reversed in a matter of microseconds. It is as if the user has taken nothing.

I'm keeping R-type close to my chest, as it is my trump card. This drug may be the only thing that keeps me alive, in a manner of speaking. I know that Leader would gladly have my head if he did not fear the distribution system that I have put in place. No one else, not even Rikoh, knows just how I was able to introduce it into an aerosol. If the population of New Eden, let alone New Earth, were to be thrust back into reality and forced to live in pain, I believe it would turn the human race into savages that even the Council could not control.

I have teamed with an amateur FleshArtist, who calls himself Andre. He will provide all the subjects I need for experimentation. We have a mutually beneficial arrangement: he provides me with test subjects, and I harvest their parts for his displays. The people believe that FleshArt is simply a way to upgrade their organs to new, healthier, bioengineered parts. No. Those parts are as flawed as the Genesis babies themselves are. Only Simon and I hold the necessary information in our genetic code to live the extended life that the Council members want. They replace their shells, their husks, every century; I am able to sustain a perfect body. I know it's more than jealousy or even survival that is at stake. To them, it is control and power. But to me, it's something else entirely—the reanimation of dead tissues, and, with Topaz's help, the complete reanimation of a once-living brain. Topaz has the key—the key to bringing the dead back to life.

Addendum:
I have just received word that Simon was horribly mutilated by some "gang" he was investigating. I was too late to stop the doctors from giving him IT, which, I fear, will make his cells rust just as his mother's did. Emily's crude form of IT caused her to leave too soon. Simon, I believe, has more time—at least a few decades. I need to get to Simon soon. Even if his cells have been compromised, I know his seed is still pure. I have had Rikoh make arrangements to bring Simon into our circle. I will not murder my nephew, but he is too important to everything I've worked for, everything I've killed for,

to let him go. He will join us. He will help in our crusade, willingly or not.

# ABOUT THE AUTHOR

A native of sunny Scottsdale, Arizona, United States of America, Thomas Milton spends his time listening to Pink Floyd records and addling his brain with all kinds of useless knowledge. He was once a mighty man, but life has made him humble…and will continue to until he gets it right.
'Blood Of New Eden' is Thomas' first published work. With influences from David Bowie, Alejandro Jordowosky, to Philip K Dick and Chuck Palahniuk, he plans to continue to entertain readers with other tales of New Earth, as well as a planned sequel to the Simon Topaz saga.

Stay Tuned for more and follow Thomas on Facebook (until his website is up!) at

www.facebook.com/thomasmiltonauthor

Oh, and if you liked (or Loathed) what you read – leave us a review on AMAZON or GOODREADS!! Psst. Tom is also MokMedia…just sayin': so expect some awesomeness to come from the MokMedia factory to be coming soon in 2018!!!

MOKHIAVELLIAN MEDIA